FREEING
FINCH

ALSO BY GINNY RORBY

FREEING FINCH

Ginny Rorby

A TOM DOHERTY ASSOCIATES BOOK

New York

FREEING FINCH

Copyright © 2019 by Ginny Rorby

Reading and activity guide copyright © 2019 by Tor Books

A Starscape Book
Published by Tom Doherty Associates
120 Broadway
New York, NY 10271

www.tor-forge.com

The Library of Congress Cataloging-in-Publication Data is available upon request.

ISBN 978-1-250-29372-5 (hardcover)
ISBN 978-1-250-29373-2 (ebook)

Our books may be purchased in bulk for promotional, educational, or business use. Please contact your local bookseller or the Macmillan Corporate and Premium Sales Department at 1-800-221-7945, extension 5442, or by email at MacmillanSpecialMarkets@macmillan.com.

First Edition: October 2019

Printed in the United States of America

0 9 8 7 6 5 4 3 2 1

Dedicated to those with
more courage than fear

and to Linda and Kate Rohr

What is the first question we ask about a newborn baby?

—*The Left Hand of Darkness,*
Ursula K. Le Guin

"Hope" is the thing with feathers -
That perches in the soul -

—Emily Dickinson

People share a common nature but are trained in gender roles.

—Lillie Devereux Blake,
novelist, essayist, and reformer

[The universe] gave us three things to make life bearable—hope, jokes and dogs, but the greatest of these was dogs.

—*Tracks,*
Robyn Davidson

PART I

CHAPTER 1

1

My name is Morgan Delgado, Junior. I was eight when Maddy Baxter, our nearest neighbor, began calling me Finch. The bird she named me after hit our front window a couple of days after my father left. It sounded like someone had thrown a clod of dirt.

Momma jumped sky-high and turned from the stove. "Jesus, Morgan, what was that?" Her hair was coming in all soft and fuzzy. "Chemo hair," she called it, curly instead of straight the way it had been before the treatments. The ceiling light made it look like she was wearing a halo.

I'd been watching TV and got up to see what happened. There was the powdery print of a bird's breast and wings against the glass. The longest feathers were outlined like angel wings, ghostly and beautiful on the pane.

I looked at Momma. "A bird hit the window."

Her eyes filled with tears. Everything made her cry back then.

I unlocked the front door. "I'm gonna go see if it's dead."

The bird lay on the deck in the blaze of light from the living room lamps. I thought for sure it was dead, but when I picked it up, little clicking sounds came from its open beak like it was struggling to breathe. I could feel its heart beating against my palm.

"Take it down to Maddy," Momma said when I came into the kitchen carrying the bird. "She'll know what to do. I'll call and tell her you're coming."

Momma held the bird against her cheek while I put on my knockoff Uggs and a coat. She handed me the bird and a flashlight from the kitchen drawer.

I clamped the flashlight in my armpit and ran down the road to Maddy's driveway with the bird cupped in my hands. Her porch light came on when I got near the house and the front door opened. Maddy is really old but knows everything there is to know about wildlife.

"Let's see what you've got." She put on her glasses.

I opened my hands and held up the coldcocked bird.

"It's a female house finch." She took it from me.

"What was it doing flying at night?"

"Something probably startled it and it flew toward the light. Were your lights on?"

"Uh-huh. Momma don't like it dark anymore."

Maddy looked at me over the tops of her reading glasses like she still has a habit of doing when there's a lesson to learn. "Doesn't like. She doesn't like it dark anymore."

I ducked my head. "It hit real hard."

Inside Maddy's kitchen, I punched holes in the lid of a shoebox with a pencil while she lined the bottom with a few clean rags. The bird looked like it was lying in a coffin before Maddy taped the lid down.

"Don't . . . doesn't it need food and water?"

"Do you eat when you're sleeping?"

"No."

"Well, then. We'll put it someplace warm and dark. If it survives the night, we'll let it go in the morning."

I trailed her to the hall closet and watched her put the shoebox on the top shelf. Rufus, one of Maddy's three cats, followed. "Not for you," Maddy said. Rufus turned and padded away.

"He acts like he understands you."

"He does. He reads my mind and I read his." Maddy closed the louvered doors.

When I got home, Momma was waiting for me on the porch. "What did she say?"

"It's a female house finch, and she thinks it will be okay." I'm not sure why I didn't tell the truth. Maddy said maybe it would die, or maybe it wouldn't.

"That's good, honey, but don't get your hopes up. It hit that window pretty hard."

"It'll be okay."

Momma was shivering. She hugged herself and rubbed her arms but took a moment to look up at the stars before following me inside.

First thing the next morning, I ran down the road to Maddy's.

"I'm glad you showed up. I'd forgotten all about that bird."

Rufus and I followed Maddy to the closet. As soon as she picked up the box, we heard the bird fluttering inside.

I grinned up at Maddy and she patted the top of my head.

"We'll test-fly her in the bathroom to make sure she doesn't have a broken wing." She shooed Rufus, who'd followed us into the small downstairs bathroom. She closed the door, then nodded for me to open the lid. The bird was standing up. She blinked at us, flew straight at the mirror, hit it lightly, and fell behind a bottle of mouthwash.

Maddy caught her and held her with the bird's neck between two middle fingers.

"Aren't you choking her?"

"Not at all. Birds have skinny little necks under all those feathers." She held her up to the light, pulled first one wing away from her body, and then the other.

"Whatcha looking for?"

"Mites. She's clean."

Maddy tested the bird's feet, which clamped down on her index finger. "The only thing wrong with this bird is she doesn't appreciate that you saved her life. Shall we?" Maddy nodded toward the door, which I opened.

In the yard, we turned to face my house. "That's the way home," Maddy said. The bird's feet were still clamped around Maddy's finger. She kissed the top of its head and moved her other hand away. The bird stayed perched as if she were as tame as a parakeet.

I held my breath. After a few seconds, I said, "Maybe she *is* hurt."

The bird looked at me, chirped once, and poof, was gone.

"Guess not." I laughed, spread my arms like I had wings, and flew in a circle around Maddy.

"One lucky bird," Maddy said. "A voice with wings." She held her hand up and we high-fived. "From now on," she said, "I think I'll call you Finch. Do you mind?"

I giggled, but shook my head. "But how come?"

Maddy shrugged. "I don't know. Maybe so every time I see you, I'll say 'Hi, Finch,' and we'll both remember this moment."

"I'm glad I didn't bring you a skunk."

Maddy laughed. "You saved a little life. Even if the bird isn't grateful, I am." She leaned and kissed the top of my head, as she'd done to the bird's before setting it free.

"Anybody would have done the same thing," I said.

"I wish that were true. You'll discover people are either givers or takers, and a good way to judge is by what they can turn their backs on."

We stood side by side, watching the chickadees mobbing the feeder on her front deck.

"I wish I could save Momma."

Maddy put her hand on my shoulder. "Your momma's fighting hard to stay here with you. That will make all the difference."

It occurred to me that Maddy hadn't asked if we'd heard from Dad.

"Why'd you really decide to call me Finch all of a sudden?"

She didn't look at me when she answered. "Sometimes I give people animal names so I can remember what they brought me that needed help."

"Not because I'm named after my dad and you hate him?" She didn't know I heard her say "good riddance" when Momma called crying to tell her she thought Daddy had left for good this time.

Maddy didn't answer.

I picked at a scab on my elbow. "It's my fault he left."

She narrowed her eyes at me. "What in the world makes you think that?"

"'Cause. You know. The thing that's wrong with me."

She knelt and hugged me. "Finch, honey, that's not the reason, and if it was, he should rot in hell."

"He told Momma she was raising a Nancy boy. What does that mean?"

"It means he's an ignorant—" Maddy's lips compressed. "Look, Finch, it's an offensive term, like calling a boy a sissy. You are not a sissy. You're a tough-as-nails little girl. I don't care that you were born a boy. Neither does your mom. It happens. There are lots of kids out in the world like you."

"There are?"

"Absolutely. Hundreds. Thousands, even. You're what you are in your head and heart, Finch, not what it says on your birth certificate."

I wanted to believe her, but thought it was just Maddy trying to make me feel not so different from other kids.

CHAPTER 2

I

I don't remember much about my mother's first battle with cancer. I was five and a half. What I do remember are like pictures in an album. Lying on my stomach outside the bathroom door listening to her throwing up. Coming home from kindergarten to see her riding our lawn mower up and down the yard wearing a flaming red wig. After the radiation treatments started, I remember walking into the bathroom and seeing her in the tub. The red wig hung on the doorknob, and the few hairs left on her head were stringy. There was a long scar where her right breast had been, and her skin, all the way to her shoulder, looked crusty brown from the radiation.

Momma opened her eyes, caught me staring, and started to cover her chest with the washcloth. But she didn't.

I said, "What did they do with the one they cut off?"

She shrugged. "I don't know, honey. Threw it away, I guess."

"Now you're half girl, half boy like me."

"We're both still girls, we're just missing a few of the parts." She reached for my hand. "When this is over, I'm going to pretend this scar is a stem." She traced it with a finger. "I'll have a rose tattooed right here." She pointed to the top of the scar. "What color shall we make it?"

"Purple," I answered.

Momma smiled. "Purple it will be."

"No, maybe red. To match your wig."

"Okay." She closed her eyes, and ladled handfuls of warm water onto her chest, avoiding the burned side.

"Momma?"

"Uh-huh?"

"Do we have any scissors?"

"Sure. There's a pair in my sewing box, and another in the drawer under the microwave." She opened her eyes and looked at me. "Why?"

"I want to cut my pee-pee off and throw it away."

"Oh, Morgan, honey." She sat up and wrapped her wet arms around me. "That would hurt terribly, sweetheart." Tears filled her eyes. "There's nothing we can do about your anatomy until you're older. You have to be patient."

"I hate it."

"I know, but promise me you'll never do anything to hurt yourself."

My father still lived with us back then. I remember his bathrobe hanging from a hook on the back of the door. "I promise," I whispered

II

They found cancer in her other breast when I was seven and a half. My most vivid memory of that time is Momma, wearing only panties, standing in front of the full-length mirror on her closet door. She looked at me and smiled a smile that didn't reach her eyes. "Now I'll be able to walk without listing to port."

"What does that mean?"

"Leaning to the left. It's a nautical term. Starboard is the right side of a boat, port the left."

"You're funny."

"I suppose so." She ran her index finger over the ridge of stitches.

After Momma got sick the second time, Dad was around less and less. She told me he'd found construction work out of town. It might have been true.

They fought a lot, often because of me. He said she was turning me into a sissy.

"My father used to call 'em Nancy boys," Daddy said, during one of those fights.

"Shame on you," Momma said, then turned and saw me standing in the kitchen doorway.

"What's a Nancy boy?" I asked.

"Nothing," Momma said. "There's no such thing."

"See." Daddy opened the refrigerator and took out a beer. "You're letting him get away with this malarkey. He needs to man up."

I was four or five when Momma told my father I was insisting I was a girl. He said I just needed a good thrashing to get that out of my system. Momma never mentioned it again, and told me it was not something we needed to discuss with my father.

Daddy put his beer on the counter and made two fists. "Put 'em up." He punched my shoulder, then jabbed the air between us and hopped from side to side.

I laughed, made fists, and danced just out of his reach.

"Jesus, son. That's what I mean. Get your thumbs out

of your fists. If you hit someone with those girly things, your thumbs will snap off at the joints like crab claws."

III

A couple weeks after my eighth birthday, Dad left and never came back, even though he promised he would. They must have gotten a divorce because less than a year later Momma met and married my stepfather, Stan. Her cancer was in remission at the time and our lives seemed normal for a while. I never understood why she had to get married, why she couldn't wait for my father to come back. That's the one thing I hold against her: she gave up on my dad too soon, then died and left me with a man who was little more than a stranger.

Maddy's told me time and again that my mother was just looking for a little happiness after everything she'd been through, but I still get angry about it—though usually only after some flare-up with Stan. Six months after their wedding, the cancer came back, this time in her bones and her liver. After that, and until she died, I practically lived at Maddy's house.

It seems I took a long time to realize Momma was going to die. I remember resenting that she couldn't get better and be there for me like a real mom. I feel guilty about that now, but back then it seemed like she could get better if she tried harder.

IV

Momma died a year and a half ago, when I was almost ten, leaving me with my stepfather. Eleven months and four days after she passed, he married Cindee. Cindee used to work at Sherwood Oaks, a local nursing home. She was also a hospice volunteer, which is how Stan met her. She helped with my mom. Now she does home health three days a week.

I liked her fine when she was taking care of Mom and didn't think much of it when Stan invited her over for dinner a couple of times after Mom died. We always told Mom stories and laughed about her mowing the yard wearing that red wig, or how she was the only person who could pick up a pill bug—"or would want to," Cindee interjected with a shudder—and not have it roll into a defensive little ball.

Cindee's the opposite of my mother, short and pudgy, bleached blonde, lots of makeup. It never crossed my mind that Stan liked her in *that way,* until he came home one night and told me they were going to Las Vegas to get married.

That I didn't ask about their trip didn't stop Cindee from getting all giggly when she told me the story. They went to a drive-through wedding chapel, both wearing sunglasses. Stan kept his foot on the brake and the engine running. The justice of the peace leaned out the window and said before he'd marry them, they'd have to take off their sunglasses and turn off the car. "This is a drive-through wedding chapel, not a drive-by."

It *was* funny, I guess, but all I could think about was, I

had just turned eleven and was now stuck with living with them until I'm eighteen unless Dad comes back. Cindee's nice enough, and Stan's okay, but I have a real father out there somewhere, and my real mother is dead.

PART II

CHAPTER 3

I

indee's at the kitchen sink with her back to me. She's plucking feathers from one of the four ducks Stan shot on his weekend hunting trip to Sacramento.

Her purse is lying open on a stool at the kitchen counter. I've just taken two crumpled bills from it when Cindee glances over her shoulder. "Want to help me with this?"

My stomach lurches, but she doesn't act like she saw me. I curl the money into my fist and put my hand in the pocket of my hoodie. "Not really."

"I don't blame you. If he shoots them, he should clean them, that's what I say."

"So why are you doing it?"

Days of Our Lives flickers on the little kitchen-counter TV set. "If I'm going to veg out in front of the television, I might as well accomplish something. Besides, I like to eat them, too, and he was so cute and happy with his kill."

"Where is Stan, anyway?"

Cindee's shoulders lift. "In the shed, I think. He was going to try to get the mower running."

"Are you working today?"

"Not until tomorrow."

"How's that old lady you're taking care of?" I open the fridge and look in. There's nothing interesting inside.

"Hanging in there."

"That's good." I close the fridge door.

"Not really. It's her time, but she doesn't trust in our Lord."

I roll my eyes. "I'm going down to the creek."

"Morgan, do you need money?" Cindee's looking at me, past her own reflection in the window over the sink.

My heart skips a beat. "No. Why?"

She smiles that rosy-cheeked smile of hers, her face framed by the hideous new white lace curtains she's hung. Momma hated anything on the windows that would block the view of the trees. "Then put it back."

"Put what back?"

She turns. "The money you took from my purse."

I take out the two bills—a one and a five—and slap them onto the counter. "I'll find him with or without your help."

I mean my real father. Between nipping a dollar here, small change there, I have about fifty dollars hidden in my room. I'm saving to go see him as soon as he writes again.

"Not by stealing money from my purse." She turns back to the sink, but she's still looking at me reflected in the window. "How long has it been since you've heard from him?"

Nearly two years ago, right after Momma died, but I'm not giving Cindee the satisfaction. "A few months."

"That's nice. Is he still in Coos Bay?"

"Yeah," I say. I don't really have a clue where he is. That two-year-old letter was postmarked Coos Bay, Oregon, but the two times I wrote trying to find him, both letters came back with yellow stickers marked undeliverable and no forwarding address. He could be anywhere, even here in town, and I wouldn't know. "Don't tell Stan about the money, okay?"

"I won't if you promise not to do it again."

My fingers are crossed behind my back. "I promise." I walk to the sink, lean, and kiss her cheek. "You're a pal."

"Morgan." She turns. "Please take the fingernail polish off before Stan notices."

I hold out my left hand and spread my fingers. It was from a bottle of Essie Blush Cindee had left in the bathroom. "I liked it on you."

"Be who God made you, okay?"

I stare at her, then shrug. "You've got a feather on your nose."

II

When I started first grade, and as long as Dad was out of town, Momma let me dress however I wanted to. I never liked dresses. Besides it's too cold in Northern California, where I live, to wear a dress without leggings. For her sake, and mine, when he was home, I hid my Little Mermaid backpack, wore my black knockoff Uggs instead of the pink ones, and covered the mermaid-tail blanket on my bed with a Spider-Man comforter.

By the time I turned eight, Dad was working nearly full-time in Oregon. When he didn't show up for my birthday in February, Momma let me get my ears pierced and I picked out Little Mermaid studs. She also let me grow my hair long enough for a ponytail.

As far as kids at school knew, I *was* a girl. The teachers and the principal knew, because "Sex: Male" is on my birth certificate. For first and second grade at Redwood Elementary, I used the girls' bathroom, but when I moved over to Dana Gray in the third grade, the principal told Mom that I needed to use the one-person-at-a-time, handicapped bathroom. By then, she'd met Stan, was finally cancer-free, and was beginning to feel better. I don't think she had it in her to fight them.

At first it didn't matter to me. Each grade had its own wing and the third's wing was closest to the only handicapped bathroom, which was in the main corridor nearly opposite the office. But fifth grade was in the wing farthest from the handicapped bathroom and my classroom was at the far end of the hall.

Didn't matter. I quit using the handicapped bathroom in the fourth grade after Amanda, a girl I don't like, saw me coming out of it. Her eyes widened, flicked to the "Handicapped" sign, and lit up. She grabbed her friend's arm. "I told you there was something wrong with her," Amanda said. The other girl giggled, and they walked away, arms linked.

From then on until I got to middle school, I either waited until I could be excused from class and use the girls' or I didn't drink anything so I didn't have to go at all.

III

I leave Cindee to her feather-plucking and cross our yard, heading for the trail to the creek. After Mom died, Stan and I put her ashes between two side-by-side redwoods that overlook a small waterfall. Stan cleared a permanent path to it for me along an old deer track, bushwhacking through the huckleberries, manzanita, and wax myrtle to where the brush ends and the Doug firs, grand firs, and ancient redwoods begin.

Mom's the one who taught me about the forest, which trees are which, why water-loving alders and redwoods grow along the creek, and Doug fir, hemlock, and grand fir on higher ground. She was an environmentalist and always tried to live a clean and healthy life, only to die of cancer at age thirty-three. I overheard someone at Mom's memorial service say, "a perfect example of the good dying young."

My walks to the creek to sit with her bring back memories of when we roamed the woods together: the chinquapin where we found a beefsteak mushroom—Mom's favorite; the woodpecker nest we discovered in the grand fir snag; the salamanders we found while gathering kindling.

I learned the trees and the birds because they were important to Mom, but since she died, I'm not as good a student as I used to be. I go to school because I have to. The middle school class I hate most is PE, where I hide in a bathroom stall to keep the other girls from seeing me change clothes.

I do like to read and often take a book down to my spot between the redwoods and read aloud to Mom, even though I can barely hear my own voice over the tumbling water. I do it because I want Mom to know I'm doing okay, and the job of mothering she did before dying was enough to last me. I don't tell her about saving up to go see my father when he writes again.

CHAPTER 4

Our house is about a half mile out on McDowell Creek Drive. We're at the top of the hill; Maddy's at the bottom where the road takes a dip before crossing the creek. Besides taking care of injured animals, Maddy paints landscapes.

I used to love going to Maddy's, not just to see what animals she had, but because she's my best friend. I don't go as often as I used to since I told her about wanting to find my father. She said not to bother and waved the notion away like a bothersome fly. She can be blunt like that, and it hurts sometimes.

The trail I use to get to the creek crosses behind her house. If I see her, I wave. Today I hear her calling.

"Hi, Finch."

Her back deck overlooks the creek and my redwoods. She's not there.

"Up here." Maddy waves from her rooftop.

"Whatcha doing?"

"Cleaning the creosote out of the chimney. My firewood was wet and now the darn thing is plugged with tar."

"Stan's home. Want me to get him to help?"

Maddy shakes her head. "No need. I do it all the time. Did you notice my new friend?"

"No."

Maddy points toward the top of her driveway. There's a large blond dog lying next to her mailbox.

"Is he yours?"

"No."

"Who owns him?"

"Not anybody who gives a flip about him. He's here twice a day since I started putting food out. Poor thing is so schizy, he'll only eat after I go back in the house. I'm sure he's been abused."

Maddy admits to liking animals much better than people. She says you can trust an animal's love. Not so much with people.

"You going down to the creek to sit with your mom?" Maddy takes the cap and spark arrester off the chimney and places them by her foot.

"Yeah."

"You're a good girl, Finch."

"I guess." Hearing her so comfortable with calling me a girl reminds me of how much I miss Mom.

II

The trail drops steeply from the point where Maddy called to me. Over the two years since Mom died, a blanket of redwood leaves has built up so it looks like a rust-colored carpet leading down to the creek.

At the base of the trail, stretching from bank to bank, is a redwood tree that fell before I was born. Its trunk is about eight feet in diameter, so big that Stan cut steps into the side of it for me with the chainsaw. I climb them, and even though the trunk is wider than a sidewalk and shows the wear of my crossings, I hold my arms out like a tight-rope walker. I'm afraid of heights, but I always stop in the middle and look down into the pool of roiling water below. It's beautiful and dangerous, but I love the feel of the mist that rises from the cascade of water.

My pair of redwoods is on the far side of the creek. They grow side by side with a space the width of Stan's La-Z-Boy recliner between them. Over the hundreds of years they've been growing there, the gap between them has col-lected a cushy pad of redwood leaves.

This is my spot. This is where Stan and I came on a warm, sunny day two years ago to put Mom's ashes so she'd always have a view of the creek and the waterfall.

I went every day to sit with her ashes, expecting to see them slowly disappear, but that's not what happened. They went just as she had, there one minute and gone the next. We had a rain, the first since she died, and when I went down to the creek the next day, her ashes were gone. I pan-icked and tried to dig down through the redwood leaves to find them, but there wasn't a trace. Now I like to believe she's part of those two trees. It helps to think she's still watching and loving me. I imagine her near the very top where the sunlight can find and warm her.

After her ashes disappeared, I began to have trouble knowing what to say. I wasn't sure she'd still be interested in the day-to-day stuff. It took me months to realize I was no longer talking to a person in pain and dying, who used to wake from a morphine-induced haze, ask me how my day had gone, and go back to sleep before I could tell her.

I've decided, if Mom *is* here, it's because she wants to hear everything. A raven lands on a redwood limb directly across the creek from me. It makes a soft gurgling sound. I click my tongue against the roof of my mouth, trying to imitate it. The raven flies off.

"Lauren's having a birthday party at the Starr Center." I don't tell Mom I'm probably not going. It's a swimming party. My bathing suit is an old one-piece with a stupid-looking skirt that probably doesn't hide enough when it's wet. "There's a new boy in school. He's really cute, but I think Amanda Ellis likes him, too."

Amanda's a snot, but I don't share stuff I think would worry Mom, like Amanda asking me last week if I was bisexual.

"Why would you say that?" I asked her.

She looked pointedly at my flat chest. "I can't tell if you're a girl or a boy."

I'm transgender. I didn't think it was the same thing as bisexual, but I walked away rather than answer. When I got home from school, I used Cindee's computer to look it up online. According to the definitions I found, bisexual is not the same thing. Amanda had it wrong, but it's scary that she'd say that. She has boobs and I don't. Most of the girls my age have them or at least the beginnings of them. Amanda's are pretty big, too.

I'm scared most of the time that, without Mom here to support me, I'll be stuck with this body I hate forever. I see boys at school who are barely older than I am and their voices are changing, some are starting to shave. I try not to think about it, but today, remembering that confrontation with Amanda, my stomach knots.

"What's going to happen to me, Momma?" suddenly spills

out. "Why'd you leave me here alone?" I close my eyes, wait-ing, praying for an answer until the silence finally gets to me. I lean back against the tree trunk and look up through its branches, then sigh. "Stan killed four ducks on his hunting trip. Cindee waits on him hand and foot, you know. I like her okay—so don't worry. They're nice to me."

I can't think of anything else to tell her. "I guess I'll go." I stroke my own cheek with the backs of my fingers the way Mom used to do every night before I fell asleep. She'd tuck me in and tell me that if I felt a warm touch during the night, it was my guardian angel checking on me while I slept.

This is a safe place for me to remember those nights. Between the trunks of my two redwoods, I can be her little girl, feel Mom's soft fingers brush my cheek like butterfly wings, and hear her whisper, "Sleep tight, pumpkin."

"Don't let the bedbugs bite," I used to say.

III

The embankment rises steeply on the other side of the creek. Out of the corner of my eye I see something move. *The breeze.* But there is no breeze. I shade my eyes. It's the dog. He's standing at the top of the trail, staring down at me.

"What?"

He's big, but thin and rangy looking, with fur the exact same color as a mountain lion's. There's a thick rope tied around his neck, and the frayed end dangles from a knot that looks chewed through. It scares me a little, the way he's staring.

"Go away." I step up onto my redwood bridge. When I look where he was, he's gone.

I cross the bridge and trudge up the hill. Off to my left I hear the sharp crack of an axe. Stan's in the state park splitting firewood again.

When he cut my trail to the waterfall, he cleared a second one into the state park that borders the west side of our property. The trail isn't much wider than the wheelbarrow he uses to enter the forest to cut up and haul out trees blown over during winter storms.

It's against the law to take anything out of a California state park, but Stan says it's stupid to leave perfectly good firewood lying around to rot, when a cord of wood, a quarter of what we need for the winter, costs three hundred dollars. He and Cindee also use the trail to go into the forest to mushroom hunt, which is also illegal. Problem is, rangers never bother with this part of Jug Handle State Park. It's long and narrow and not linked to any of the rest of the park. Maddy's our only neighbor, but she either doesn't know what Stan is doing, or if she does, she keeps quiet about it. Stan calls her a live-and-let-live neighbor.

CHAPTER 5

'm about to enter the dense trees that block the view of Maddy's house from ours when I sense I'm being watched again. I turn. The dog's on the path between the two rows of cages where Maddy keeps whatever she's rehabbing. He whines, tucks his tail, runs a few feet, stops, looks back, and whines again.

"I'm not in charge of you. Go nag Maddy." I glance at her roof. She hasn't replaced the wire-mesh spark arrester or the chimney cap.

I helped her clean the chimney once, so I figure she's probably downstairs scooping the dislodged creosote into a bucket.

Stan comes onto the trail ahead of me. He's pushing a wheelbarrow full of freshly split wood. "That downed fir will keep us warm all winter."

Downed my butt. He took it down, and it's the grand fir the pileated woodpecker nested in the year before Mom died.

"How'd your visit go?" he says.

I'm not sure why I resent his asking. I don't for a second think he cares. He's hasn't gone to see Mom since the day we spread her ashes. If he'd really loved her, he'd pay his respects once in a while, and he'd have waited longer before marrying Cindee.

"Okay."

"Did she have anything to say?"

I look at him sharply, but he's repositioning a log that's threatening to slip off the pile.

"Are you making fun of me?"

He looks surprised. "Not at all." He tilts his head back and sniffs the air like a dog. "I smell duck roasting."

II

All during dinner, my mind keeps returning to the spark arrester on Maddy's chimney. I used to help my father clean our chimney by knocking off the creosote that built up on the wire mesh. Maddy wouldn't risk making a fire in the woodstove without cleaning or replacing the arrester and the chimney cap.

"Cindee's not your maid," Stan says when I get up from the table without taking my plate to the sink.

I roll my eyes, take my plate and Cindee's, but not Stan's.

The landline phone is beside the refrigerator. It's been so long since I've called Maddy, I have to get the phone book out and look up her number. No answer. That's doubly weird. Maddy rarely goes out at night because she can't see to drive after dark. Night blindness, she calls it.

"Have you got homework?" Stan asks.

"I'm going down to Maddy's first."

"Why?" Cindee says.

"I don't know. I have a bad feeling."

"Call her," Stan says, as if I weren't smart enough to have thought of that already.

"I just did. There's no answer."

Cindee gets up, stands behind Stan, and begins massaging his shoulders. "She's probably out feeding her critters."

"She doesn't feed them after dark." She does have an owl, Otus, but she feeds him during the day, and Ravenous, a red-tailed hawk, isn't nocturnal.

"Doesn't she play bridge every night of the week with that clutch of old crones she hangs with?" Stan rotates his head. "That feels good." He reaches around and pats Cindee's butt.

Yuck. Maddy *does* play a lot of bridge, but not every night. "I'm still going to check on her."

"It's dark. Stan, you go with him." Cindee slaps his shoulder lightly.

"It'll take me five minutes." I don't need him.

Cindee goes to the junk drawer where they keep batteries, rubber bands, twist ties, and multiple half-used tubes of Krazy Glue. She fishes out a small LED penlight. "Are you going on the trail or the road?"

"Road. Why?"

"Wear my white sweater so cars can see you. And walk facing traffic."

"It's a hundred yards."

"For me. Okay?"

I shrug, take her cardigan off the hook by the door, and put it on over the shirt and my fleece vest. Cindee is almost as round as she is tall. I'm five-five and spindly. The sweater is huge on me.

The night is crystal clear. An airplane winks across the

sky. On nights like this, Mom and I would sometimes pull the hammock from under the trees, huddle together in our sleeping bags, and fall asleep watching for shooting stars.

There are no streetlights this far out of town. I turn onto the dark road, but don't bother with the flashlight. I've walked this short piece of pavement a thousand times.

From far down the road, I hear a car coming. I walk a little faster, my breath coming in misty puffs. I turn into Maddy's driveway and dodge behind a tree so the lights won't hit me when the car crests the hill. I like the idea of watching it pass without the driver knowing I'm here.

I see the dog caught in the momentary flash of the car's headlights. He's lying in the lower driveway next to Maddy's car. I turn on the penlight and wish it were brighter. Another car is coming. I stay hidden behind the tree and watch for its lights to expose the dog again. By the time it passes, the dog has disappeared. Maddy said his routine is to eat and leave. What's he still doing here?

Maddy has an upper driveway and a lower driveway. If it's supposed to rain, she parks in the carport on the upper level because her sunroof leaks and she can get into the house through the back door to her bedroom without getting wet. The rest of the time, she parks on the lower level, near her front door, which is where the car is. It's only eight thirty, too early for her to be asleep, but there are no lights on in the house. Maybe she *is* out playing bridge, but she wouldn't have gone and not fed the dog.

From the upper driveway, I shine the thin flashlight beam at the chimney. The cap and screen are still missing, and there's no smoke, so no fire in the woodstove. I go into the carport and knock on the back door. The only sounds, besides the muted tumble of the waterfall, are

Maddy's red-tailed hawk shaking itself to redistribute its feathers, and the short murmuring call of Otus, her ten-year-old screech owl.

Suddenly every nerve in my body tells me what's wrong. "Maddy!" I run to the stairs that connect the upper-level driveway to the lower and take them down three at a time. "Maddy, where are you?" I shout.

Nothing. Not a sound.

"Maddy?" I round the front side of the house and trip over her. She's lying half on, half off the walkway. Her body is on the walk, but her head is under a large hydrangea. She's landed on her side, and her left arm is twisted at an odd angle.

Maddy moans and opens her eyes. "Finch?"

"It's me."

"Oh, Finch. Thank God. I'm so cold."

I kneel beside her. "Let me help you up."

"I can't. My hip and arm are broken. Call 911."

I step over her and try the door. "It's locked, Maddy."

She doesn't answer.

"Maddy?"

"There's a ladder in the carport." Her voice is barely a whisper. "Use it to get onto the roof. The sliding glass door to my bedroom is open."

I start across the front deck, then run back, pull off Cindee's sweater, and put it across Maddy's shoulder.

"Thanks, honey," she whispers.

I race up the steps, lug the ladder down to the landing, open it, and lock the two crossbars. I climb high enough to step up onto the narrow edge of the roof that extends beyond the deck. It's only about a foot wide and steep, so I hold on to the upright bars of the deck railing and don't look down. The gate in the railing is open. I cross the deck, turn on a light, and search frantically for a phone. There isn't one. I know where the downstairs phone is; I used it a million times to call home and check on my mother.

I run down the stairs, grab the cordless phone off Maddy's messy desk, and dial 911. As it rings, I grab the throw off the sofa, unlock the front door, and turn on the porch light.

While we wait for the ambulance, Maddy drifts in and out of consciousness. I'm glad. When she's awake the pain she's in is horrible. It reminds me of Mom toward the end; she moaned even in her sleep.

Town is only four miles away. I begin to hear the siren pretty soon after I call and, a few minutes later, hear the ambulance turn onto McDowell Creek Drive. "They're coming, Maddy."

I can tell by how fast they're driving they aren't going to slow down in time to make the driveway. A second later the ambulance wails by, lights flashing.

McDowell Creek dead-ends about a mile past Maddy's. They have to come back this way. After covering Maddy with the throw from the sofa, I'd put Cindee's sweater back on. Now I strip it off and run up the driveway. When the wailing grows louder and I see the flashing red lights bounce off the trees, I turn on the penlight and wave the white sweater.

The paramedic pats my shoulder. "Are you her granddaughter?"

I feel a momentary shock at being recognized as a girl. "A neighbor," I say.

"Don't worry too much. She'll be fine, but she's very lucky you found her." He closes the first side of the ambulance doors.

Maddy lifts her head. "Take care of my animals, Finch."

"I will, Maddy."

"And don't forget the dog."

CHAPTER 6

I

fter the ambulance leaves, I turn out the lights and lock the house with the spare key Maddy keeps on the mantel. I shine the flashlight around looking for the dog, but he's either gone or lurking in the dark somewhere. Maybe he was trying to get me to follow him earlier this afternoon—show me that Maddy had fallen. I'll never know.

here have you been?" Stan demands. "I've been calling that house for an hour."

I don't answer. He's exaggerating. Maddy's phone was in my vest pocket. It never rang.

"You gonna answer me?" Stan says.

"Maddy fell. Didn't you hear the ambulance?"

"We had the music on pretty loud," Cindee says.

"Fell where?" Stan says.

"Off the roof. She'd been lying there for hours."

"Oh, that poor old thing." Cindee clasps her hands together. "How bad is she hurt?"

"Pretty bad. She broke an arm and her hip."

"That's not good," Cindee tells Stan. "Old people who break hips often die. My grandmother did."

"She's not old and she won't die," I snap. Because Cindee's a nurse's aide, she thinks she knows everything.

"Of course she won't, sweetie," Cindee says. "My grandmother was a lot older than Maddy. How old is she, anyway?"

Stan shrugs. His head is back and he's putting Visine in his eyes.

I know, but I'm not telling Cindee. This summer Maddy and I drove a bunch of baby swallows to a rehab center in Petaluma, and she got stopped for speeding. I dug her driver's license out of her purse for her. She's sixty-six.

"I'll pray for her tonight," Cindee chirps. "You have to let go and let God." Cindee's eyes glisten with tears.

"Been there," I mumble.

I prayed my heart out for my mother to live and—if God exists—he let her die anyway. Cindee's answer to everything is to put it in God's hands, like she did when Stan lost his security job at the old Georgia-Pacific mill site. She's convinced God will provide him with a new one. He must believe it, too, because he hasn't bothered looking for another.

I once asked her if everything is God's will, how come I'm a girl in a boy's body? "God doesn't make mistakes, Morgan. It's a phase. You'll grow out of it," Cindee said.

I've always felt like a girl. "If it's a phase, I'm at eleven and a half years and counting," I said.

If I was going to pray for anything ever again, it would be to find my father. I'd try to be a boy for him.

I go into the kitchen, open the refrigerator door, and stare at the contents. There's a carton of orange juice, but when I reach for it, my hand starts to shake, and the backs of my knees tingle.

"Morgan?" Cindee's voice is far away. "Morgan." Cindee pats my shoulder.

I open my eyes. Stan is holding a wet dish towel, and it's dripping into a puddle of orange juice beside my head. Cindee helps me sit up.

"What happened?"

"You fainted."

"I was reaching for the juice and thinking, if Maddy . . ." I stop.

If Maddy dies, I'll have no one.

II

That night, I set my alarm to get up an hour earlier. I'll need time to feed Maddy's animals before school. At the moment, she only has her permanent residents: Otus, her owl; Ravenous, a cranky red-tailed hawk, nicknamed Rav; her cats; and now that creepy-acting dog. At least it's not like summer, when people bring her baby birds that have left the nest too early, or fallen to the ground, or been caught by a cat. Those Maddy raises and releases—except the swallows. Baby swallows have to be taught how to catch insects by adult birds, so Maddy raises them until they can fly, then drives them to the rescue center in Petaluma.

I always go with her. Baby birds get hungry every twenty minutes, and the drive is two and a half hours. Last summer there'd been eight babies to feed—four barn swallows and four cliff swallows.

I loved dropping mealworms into their gaping beaks. As babies, their beaks are ringed with rubbery yellow skin that, with the dandelion-like puffs of down on the tops of their heads, makes them look like frowning, crabby old men. But what I liked best about feeding baby birds was the soft, chirpy, hiccupy sound they make when they're full.

Maddy uses Otus, who is blind in one eye, and Rav in her educational programs at local schools. She starts by telling kids that, with few exceptions, every animal she ends up with is there because of something a human did to hurt it. Rav is an example. He has only one wing. The other was splintered by a hunter's buckshot and had to be amputated.

There's a small freezer in Maddy's carport where she keeps the frozen mice and baby chicks she feeds to Otus and Rav. I get two mice out of the freezer, one for each of them, lay them aside to defrost, and go down to feed her three cats.

The two females—Risty, a calico, and Cory, a black-and-white tuxedo cat—don't like anyone except Maddy, but they know me well enough not to run and hide. Both are sitting in the bay window when I unlock the front door, like they're watching for Maddy to come home. Rufus, who is yellow and old, is asleep in front of the Monitor heater.

Cory and Risty jump down, run to their empty dishes, and start to meow. Maddy must have fallen before she got a chance to feed them last night, and I didn't think to do it after the ambulance left.

The remains of three cans of food are in the fridge, which means Maddy is still catering to their individual likes and dislikes. There's beef, fish, and senior diet for Rufus. I fill the dry-food bowl, clean the dry bits of yesterday's breakfast from their dishes, empty the three cans into their separate bowls, and leave it to them to sort out who eats what.

I clean the litter box, put seed in the bird feeders, and get a half dozen mealworms out of a container in the fridge for Otus. I lock the house and am headed across the front deck when I see the dog. He's sitting at the top of the driveway, watching me.

I make a U-turn and go back into the house for a dish. I open all the cabinet doors until I find a bag of kibble under the sink.

"Here." I set the bowl on the deck, thinking it's too bad Maddy started feeding him in the first place. It only encourages him to hang around. I use the water in a rain barrel to fill another bowl with water and put it beside his food dish.

The dog lies with his front paws stretched out in front of him and his head up. He looks a little like pictures of the Sphinx in Egypt.

"Suit yourself," I say. "The jays and ravens will eat it if you don't."

There are six walk-in cages on the little rise above Maddy's carport, three on either side of a center path. They are plywood on three sides with evenly spaced thin wooden lath slats in front. Hardware cloth lines the inside of the lath to keep rodents out and small birds from escaping through the slats. The dimensions and design are dictated by the California Department of Fish and Wildlife, from which Maddy has a permit to rehabilitate wildlife.

I open Otus's cage and step inside. Otus has always liked me and seems to remember I used to feed him. He bobs his head trying to focus his one good eye and makes little snapping sounds with his beak before flying to land on my head. His talons are sharp and his grip painful. I put the defrosted mouse on the redwood stump in the middle of his cage, scrape him off, and set him beside it. He must be lonely because he ignores his mouse and flies to the top of my head again. I lift him off, put him on my shoulder, and give him a mealworm. He takes it, flies to one of his perches, eats it, and flies back to the top of my head.

"I don't have time to play with you." I take him off again and bribe him to stay on the redwood stump with two mealworms. I change his water and give him the last of the worms to make my escape.

Unlike Otus, Rav doesn't like me at all. He isn't too crazy about Maddy, either, but he'll come down off his perch for food. That's how Maddy catches and hoods him for the trips to schools, where he stares at students with menacing yellow eyes. He probably holds a grudge against humans for shooting him out of the sky. One minute he was soaring, drifting in effortless circles, and the next he tumbled to earth. I'd be mad, too.

When I slip into his cage, every feather on his head and shoulders rises threateningly. Something about Rav reminds me of my grandfather, and I feel sorry for him.

My mom's dad was like that, using anger to keep some control over his life after he lost first one leg then the other to diabetes. He took every act of kindness as patronizing. It even made him mad when someone held a door for him. But inconsiderate people, who didn't hold a door, infuriated him.

Mom and I would pick him up at the Sherwood Oaks Nursing Home every Sunday and take him to breakfast at the Home Style Café. He got mad at one person for driving too fast, another for driving too slow, and at teenagers for playing their car stereos so loud your chest vibrated. But people who threw trash out their windows topped his hate list. He said the world was full of people who thought the planet revolved around them. "Don't grow up thinking the world owes you a living," he told me, shaking a bony finger in my face. "It owes you nothing."

"I won't, Papaw," I'd say.

Maddy has hung a series of branches, placing each within jumping distance of the other, so Rav can reach his food. He cries loudly when I enter and hops to the top branch, one wing spread and the nub of the other held out for balance. He glares at me as if I'm to blame for his limitations.

Before putting a mouse on his feeding platform, I change his water. He'll come down instantly for his breakfast, and I don't want him to have to work his way back up when I return with clean water.

Before leaving, I peek through the slats of the other four cages to make sure I haven't missed a new arrival. They're empty.

I wait until I'm hidden by the trees to look back at the dog. He's coming down the driveway, head low, tail tucked. He looks pitiful, and I watch him start to eat before I take the trail home to get ready for school.

CHAPTER 7

I

Amanda is in the back of the bus with her clutch of friends. I take a seat near the front behind Rita, another of Amanda's targets. Rita is the biggest girl in school but fights back against bullies by dressing outrageously and dyeing her hair different colors. I wish I had her nerve. But then, what do I know? She may be dying inside, too.

At the next-to-last stop on Sequoia Road, an old red Mustang convertible pulls up behind the bus, and the driver guns the motor. When the bus driver folds the stop arms, the Mustang pulls out and roars past. A girl with streaks of electric blue in her hair is driving. Her passenger's wearing a hoodie.

"Another kid with a death wish," the bus driver says.

When we arrive at school, I pick up my backpack and stand, but Amanda blocks my way to the aisle. "How many cat shirts do you have?"

I'm wearing my black shirt with rows of white cat faces, denim shorts, black leggings, and my light blue Converse high-top All Stars. "I don't know. Why?"

"Didn't you wear it yesterday?" Amanda sneers. She's trying to look disgusted, but if she ever saw what that look does to her face she'd never do it again.

I probably did. "No."

"Eww! You did, too." She shoves past me.

Her friends laugh.

II

I'm slouched in my desk watching Amanda, who is two rows in front of me, gluing glitter on the boy's name she's written inside her notebook. She blows the excess onto the floor, leaving GABE to sparkle. He's the new kid.

Lauren, who is the nicest girl in school, glances at me and smiles. She and I used to be friends when Mom was alive and would drive me to parties. I think we'd still be friends if I lived closer to town.

The final bell rings and Ms. Dixon clears her throat. "Let's get started."

The classroom door opens and in strolls the passenger from the Mustang. She's still got the hood up on her sweatshirt.

"Yes?" Ms. Dixon says.

"I'm Sherri Vines." She hands our teacher a piece of paper.

Ms. Dixon looks at it and then at Sherri. "You're enrolling this late in the year?"

"We just moved here from Nevada." She shrugs. "I'll do the best I can."

"No hoodies in my classroom."

"Sorry." She pushes the hood back, exposing streaks of electric blue to match the girl driving. "My sister had the top down in the car."

"There's a seat in the back."

"Thank you." She has a southern accent and walks like there's a red carpet to the back of the room.

Amanda's mouth actually hangs open. After Sherri sits down, Amanda whispers something to Lacey, whose desk is in front of mine. Lacey giggles and looks at Sherri.

Sherri straightens in her chair and stares so hard at Amanda that Amanda swallows and turns to face the front.

"Take out your journals," Ms. Dixon says. "We write in our journals each morning, Ms. Vines. You may use notebook paper for now."

I glance at Sherri again. I have a feeling Amanda has made an enemy of the wrong person this time.

III

I wanted to go see Maddy after school, and Cindee agreed to come into town to pick me up at the hospital at four thirty; that will give me an hour to visit. I called Maddy yesterday, but she was too groggy to say more than a few words, none of which made sense.

It's about two miles to the hospital, and though the route is different from the middle school than it was from Dana Gray Elementary, walking there is all too familiar. When Mom was in for the last time, I walked it every day. Stan was still a guard at the closed-down Georgia-Pacific mill site, so it was Maddy who picked me up and took me home after my visits.

The volunteer at the reception desk looks up when I come through the automatic door. I don't recognize her. Two years ago, I knew them all.

"May I help you?"

"Maddy Baxter's room, please?"

She types Maddy's name in the computer. "Room 109. Go left, then—"

"I know the way. Thanks."

The second time Mom got cancer, she was in room 105. I remember walking down this hall. On my right is the same bulletin board with cheery, uplifting messages and employee tributes. On my left, at the end of the hall, is the tiny cafeteria full of vending machines where I'd sit and wait for Maddy to drive up.

I pass 105. The door is closed. When I reach 109, I tap lightly and push it open.

Maddy's eyes are closed. Her left arm is in a cast. There's the sound of something inflating. Her left leg lifts a little, then a hissing sound as it lowers again. I cross the room and sit in the chair. Air whooshes out of the seat cushion.

A bag of clear liquid hangs from a rod and drips slowly into a tube that ends at a needle stuck into the top of Maddy's right hand. Seeing it makes the back of my knees tingle.

The minutes tick by. "Maddy?" I whisper.

I told Cindee 4:30 at the main entrance. It's 3:50. I sit for a while longer, listening to the sounds of the machines in the room. During my mother's last stay, I'd sit by her bed for hours watching her chest rise and fall. By then I was nearly ten and knew she was going to die. Watching Maddy breathe reminds me of how I used to watch that thin, black hand on the clock skip to the next minute, and then the next, and how I willed it to hold still, stop eating away, chewing and swallowing, what remained of my mother's life.

"Hi, Finch."

She startles me and I jump. "Hi, Maddy."

"Remembering your mom?"

"Uh-huh. How you doing?"

"Pretty good, sweetie, considering. How are the critters?"

"They're fine. Otus is lonesome. I have to leave him extra mealworms so he'll let me out of the cage."

Maddy laughs, then grimaces with pain. "He's spoiled. How's the dog?"

"Fine, I guess."

"I'm so curious about him." Her voice fades and her eyes close.

The smells, sounds, and the squeaking of the nurses' rubber-soled shoes are too much like when Mom was here. I want to take Maddy's wrinkled, spotted hand and press it to my cheek, but am too shy, even with Maddy, to do it.

"Are you asleep?"

"No."

"You must have fallen right after I was there."

"Not five minutes after you disappeared down the hill," she says without opening her eyes.

"How did that happen?"

"Sheer stupidity." She turns her head to look at me. "I took the chimney cap off and put it next to my foot, then accidentally kicked it. I tried to grab it before it rolled off the roof. I rolled off instead."

"I'm sorry. I shoulda checked earlier."

"As it was, you saved my life."

"No, I didn't."

"Yes, you did. If I'd lain there all night, I don't think I would have made it to morning. What made you come down?"

"I noticed the spark arrester and the chimney cap were missing. That, and the dog kept hanging around watching me. None of it felt right."

Maddy shakes her head and flinches. "I'm sure in a fix, aren't I?"

I nod. "The animals miss you."

"You may have to keep the feeding up for quite a while. Can you do that?"

"Sure."

"I'll pay you."

"You don't have to do that."

"If it weren't you, I'd be paying someone else. Might as well keep it in the family." She pats my hand.

I shrug, but I'm thinking, this means, if I find out where my dad is, I may be able to go see him even sooner.

"Dr. Rohr did my hip replacement this morning. If all goes well, I can leave at the end of next week, but God only knows when I can come home."

"Where will you go?"

"Sherwood Oaks."

"That's for really old people." I think of my grandfather. "Why do you have to go there?"

"I have to rehab my new hip. How's that for irony? I'm the critter with broken parts now." Her eyes close.

CHAPTER 8

"How's she doing?" Cindee asks when I get in the car.

"Okay, but she's not going to be home for a while. She has to go to Sherwood Oaks to learn to walk with her new hip."

"I used to work there, remember? It's a nice place—as far as places like that go."

"Why'd you quit, then?"

"Home health gives me more flexible hours. We thought it was kind of important that I stay home as much as I could."

"What for?"

She shrugs. "I don't know. In case you needed a friend." She smiles.

I turn and look out the window. Sometimes I have to really work hard not to like Cindee. And the way she said it, with a hint of sadness in her tone, makes me wonder if Cindee wishes we *were* friends like Maddy and I are.

At home, I get out to check the mail. Even after a year and a half, I'm still the first to the mailbox, always hoping there will be a letter or maybe a card from my father. Today, it's the usual junk, which I hand through the car window to

Cindee. "I'm going down to feed the animals." I turn and call over my shoulder, "Thanks for picking me up."

"You're welcome. We're having leftover duck for dinner."

"It was good."

Cindee flips down the sun visor to check her lipstick. "How do I look?"

I shrug. "It's just Stan."

"Gotta look good for my man."

I want to throw up.

||

I crest the hill down to Maddy's and coming from the other direction is the dog. About the time I see him, I hear a car coming. Too many people at the far end of McDowell Creek drive like maniacs, hitting the top of the hill fast enough to sail up the other side. The dog is walking the pavement at the edge of the right lane.

"Get off the road!" I shout.

The dog looks up and stops.

The car is coming, and the driver guns it to pick up speed for the hill.

"Get off the road!" I scream, wave my arms, and start to run.

Instead of getting out of the way, the dog turns like he's heading back up the hill to escape me. He's running in the right lane.

Tires squeal.

I cover my eyes.

The driver blasts his horn as he passes in a spray of gravel and exhaust.

"You idiot!" I scream at him and turn, expecting to see the dog dead in the road.

He's standing in a patch of weeds.

"You're an idiot, too!" I shout. My heart whooshes in my ears. "Come eat." I cross to Maddy's driveway.

At her mailbox, I stop and call the dog again.

He sits.

"Look, I'm sorry I yelled at you. You scared me." I pat my thigh. "Come get dinner."

He doesn't budge.

I feed the cats and go to check on Otus and Rav. Otus has vomited up a pellet of fur and mouse bones. Maddy collects these for her education programs, to show kids how owls swallow their prey whole, then throw up the parts they can't digest. I take it to save.

The last thing I do is put a dish of food out for the dog, who's now lying at the top of Maddy's driveway. He scratches at the rope around his neck, then lowers his head to rest it on top of his paws.

"Better eat this before those ravens get it." Two of them are strutting around the yard near the compost heap.

On the trail home, I step behind a tree to watch the dog come down the driveway and begin to eat.

What is *your story?*

CHAPTER 9

I

The new girl, Sherri, is like watching a movie star or seeing a bad accident. She's hard to look away from. She's pretty, but so are lots of girls. I'm not sure if she's any older than the rest of us, but she seems more so-phisticated. Maybe because she's been to more places. I envy that she doesn't seem to care that Amanda and her crowd don't like her and whisper behind her back. Even boys who pretend to hate girls turn to watch Sherri when she walks by. Best of all, Gabe—the boy Amanda likes—who ignores every attempt by Amanda to get his attention, was talking and laughing with Sherri in the cafeteria line at lunch yesterday. I loved it because Amanda was stomping mad.

I'm waiting at the bus stop after school Thursday when I hear Amanda and Lacey giggling. "Hey, Broomstick," Amanda says, and turns to Lacey. "I see you're still using the handicapped bathroom."

"Less chance of running into you in there," I say. My stomach knots. I made the mistake of having a Coke at lunch and couldn't wait. I took the chance no one would see me. When I came out, the only kid in the hall was Amanda. She grinned from ear to ear.

Sherri's leaning against the school-zone sign, waiting for her sister like she does every day. She looks over when Amanda speaks.

Amanda holds her arm out to stop Lacey from getting any closer. "Be careful. Whatever Morgan's got may be catching."

Sherri pushes off the sign and walks over. "Morgan, right?"

"Uh-huh." This is my chance to begin ridding myself of my boy name. "But my friends call me Finch."

"What friends?" Amanda says.

If Sherri heard her, she doesn't show it. "Love it," she says. "I'm waiting for my sister. Mind if I stand with you?"

I shake my head and side-eye Amanda. She's moved away and is leaning against a red Prius.

"Thanks," I say to Sherri.

"What for?"

"You know." I nod in Amanda's direction. "I'm not sure why she hates me."

"Why would you care?"

I shrug. She's right, I don't know why I care. "I like your accent. Are you from the South?"

"I was born in Houston."

"I saw you and your sister behind our bus on Monday. You must live near me."

"Mom's moved us in with her new boyfriend. It's a dumpy little place on Sequoia."

"I live off Sequoia, on McDowell."

"That's cool. Want a ride home? My sister won't mind."

"It's past your house."

"By what? A half mile? You want to ride in that stinky

bus with her?" She hitches a thumb in Amanda's direction. "Or be chauffeured?"

"Let's see." I pretend to struggle with the decision.

Sherri's laugh is exaggerated—as if I'd said something really funny.

"How old are you?" I ask.

She glances at Amanda and cups a hand to her mouth. "Thirteen in January," she whispers. "How 'bout you?"

"Twelve in February," I whisper back.

"You're tall."

"I know. I'm a beanpole." I hold my arms away from my sides.

"I wish I was taller. You'll always be nice and thin."

Sherri's shorter than me, but has a real figure, with boobs and a small waist.

"How come you're not in the seventh grade?" I ask.

"I started late, then got held back once with all the moving we've done. First Houston, then L.A., Portland, Vegas, and now here. I hope this is it, but—" She shakes her head. "—it never is."

"How come so many times?"

Sherri shrugs. "Mom meets some dude online and we follow him for a while, then she meets someone else, and off we go again. This new one, Jake, is from here."

We hear tires squeal and both turn. Her sister leaves a streak of rubber and a puff of exhaust as the red Mustang peels off from the stop sign on the corner, does a U-turn, and pulls into the School Bus Only lane.

"I love your car."

"It's my mom's."

"You and your sister look like twins."

"We're not. She's sixteen—" She grins. "—almost."

"You can drive at fifteen in Nevada?"

Sherri covers her mouth again so no one will hear her. "Her license says she's sixteen."

She introduces me to her sister, Deanne, who nods and continues to bob her head in time with the music. I climb into the back. It's freezing with the top down, but it beats a bus ride home with Amanda.

About a quarter of a mile before the turnoff on McDowell, Sherri points out where they live. It *is* a dump. The yard is littered with two broken-down cars, plastic chairs, and an empty chain-link cage.

I ask to be dropped at Maddy's, with the excuse that I need to feed the animals, but really so Cindee and Stan don't see me. I don't feel like being interrogated about my new friend.

Sherri says, "We can give you a ride to school every morning if you want."

I look at Deanne.

"Take the bus to our house," her sister says. "We'll wait for you."

"That would be great." I climb out. "Maddy has an owl and a hawk. I could show you sometime."

"Awesome," Sherri says. "We love animals, but we move around too much to have a pet."

||

After I finish feeding the birds and cats and put out food for the dog, I pretend to leave for home. Instead, I sit on a tree stump near where the trail enters the woods, and watch the dog lick the bowl. After he starts up the driveway, I wait until he's past where the creek spills through the culvert before leaving my hiding place. I keep as far back as I can, waiting for him to round a bend before running to catch sight of him again. It's all uphill, so I have to stop when I reach the curve and put my hands on my knees to let my breathing slow.

The dog is a few hundred yards ahead, walking slowly, sniffing, and occasionally lifting his leg to pee. Twice he stops, sits, and digs at the rope around his neck with a hind foot. I wait until he disappears around the next bend before following.

My guess is I've gone less than half a mile when the road straightens out and starts to climb. I reach the top of the hill before I see the dog again. He's almost to the point where the road turns sharply left. I hear a car coming. I step off to the side of the road and stand waiting for it to pass. Behind me on the wooded slope down to a branch of the creek are discarded mattresses, bottles, and other garbage. The car crests the hill, going fast. The driver, a kid, blasts his horn at me.

I step out onto the road. When I look up, the dog has stopped and is watching me. I will him to keep going and walk along casually, as if we're just coincidentally headed in the same direction. I stop to examine a cow parsnip bloom that's nearly as tall as I am, and when I glance to see if the dog is still watching, he's disappeared.

It takes me another five minutes to reach where I last spotted him, but he's not ahead of me or on the road at all. I try whistling for him even though I know it's hopeless.

At least the walk back to Maddy's is mostly downhill.

CHAPTER 10

I

The next day, I board the school bus in front of Maddy's house at 7:10. When it stops opposite their house ten minutes later, Sherri and Deanne are sitting in their mother's car at the end of the driveway. Sherri waves.

"Where do you think you're going?" the driver asks when I get out of my seat and stand at the front waiting for the kids to finish loading.

"My friends are driving me today. See?" I point to the red Mustang.

The driver cranes her neck to look out the window. "I don't know about that."

Sherri waves again and smiles. Deanne holds up her wrist and taps where a watch would be if she wore one. Traffic in both directions is building up. The driver glances in the rearview mirror. When the last kid boards, I hop off.

As the bus pulls away, I see Amanda and her friends staring out the window. They look like fish in an aquarium.

Sherri and I are standing by the water fountain outside

the Language Arts classroom when I see Amanda and Lacey coming down the hall.

"Hey, Morgan, you gonna introduce me to your new pal?" Lacey says.

"Did you forget?" Amanda says. "Her name is Starling now, or is it Pigeon?" Amanda smiles at Sherri.

For a second it crosses my mind that Sherri might like to be friends with her. She's popular; I'm not.

Sherri lifts her chin and stares down her nose at Amanda. "If you need to interrupt when I'm talking to my friend, say 'excuse me.'"

Amanda blinks like she's been slapped.

"And," Sherri adds, "if I ever decide I want to know who you are, I'll ask."

My insides light up.

II

Stan's usually up early and out in the state park forest doing something he shouldn't be doing, like cutting down a tree or looking for mushrooms to sell. I'm getting ready for school in the hall bathroom, which is mine since Stan and Cindee took Mom's room. I'm dressed except for my leggings and am sitting on the toilet when the door opens.

"Oops, sorry." Stan pulls the door closed. I hear, "What the hell?" and the door flies open again. He storms in, grabs my wrist, and drags me out of the bathroom. I'm wearing a pair of Mom's panties. They slip from my thighs to my ankles.

"Let go!" I try to wrench my hand free.

"What's going on?" Cindee's in the kitchen in her pink robe and matching fuzzy slippers.

"Nothing," Stan snaps.

Halfway across the living room, the panties trip me. I land on my knees.

Stan pulls me to my feet with a grip on my wrist so tight the blood pools in my hand. He grabs me around the waist, hoists me onto one hip, and carries me the rest of the way. I kick off the panties, so I can run when he puts me down. He opens the door, hauls me across the deck and out into the yard.

"Stan? What are you doing?" Cindee runs after us. "Let him go."

With his free hand, he unzips his fly. "I caught him sitting on the toilet like a girl. I'm going to show him how men pee."

I beat on him with my fists.

He puts me down but holds me in place by my ponytail while he pees on the roses by the front step.

I fight back tears. "I'm not a boy." I take a swing and hit his arm.

Cindee comes down the steps, knocks Stan's hand away, and puts her arm around my shoulders. "Shame on you," she says to him. "What were you thinking? He's only eleven and it's not our—" She doesn't finish. "It's a stage he's going through."

Stan lets me go and zips his fly. "His mother let him get away with this I'm-a-girl crap. And he was wearing her underpants, long hair, fingernail polish. It's disgusting." He shakes a finger in my face. "It's time for you to man up."

"I *am* a girl." The words come out in a strangled little bark. "Maddy believes me."

"That old lady's gonna croak one day and *we'll* be all you've got."

"Stan. Shut up." Cindee's tone is one I've never heard before—like she's more scared than mad.

I hear the school bus driver slow at the stop across from Maddy's. She sees I'm not there and guns the engine to make it up the hill. It rumbles by our house a moment later.

Cindee digs a Kleenex out of her robe pocket and hands it to me. "Blow your nose and go finish dressing." She hands me my panties and begins pulling the bobby pins from those dumb-looking curls that frame her face. "I'll take you to school."

"I'm not going to school." I dodge away from Stan when he makes a grab for my arm and take off running. When I reach the road, I turn and shout, "I'm a girl, and I was try-ing to poop!"

I want to go to Mom and my trees, but if Stan comes after me, that's where he'll look first. I head for Maddy's, but opposite her house, I cross McDowell and take a deer track into the woods.

Dressed only in a T-shirt, flannel shirt, and Mom's un-derwear, I sit on a log by the creek, hating Stan until my teeth start to chatter. I'm up the creek a few yards from the culvert that runs under the road. It amplifies the sound of the water flowing through to Maddy's side. As loud as it is, I can still hear the scream of Stan's chainsaw start up.

I climb the trail to the road. The dog is by Maddy's mail-box, watching the house. I've forgotten the animals. They must be starving.

"Hi, dog." My voice is soft to warn but not scare him.

He shoots straight into the air, flees down Maddy's driveway, and disappears into her woods.

"Please come back," I whisper, and begin to shiver.

I don't know why, but last week I started hiding Maddy's house key. I'd been leaving it on my dresser at home. Nothing happened to make me decide to hide it, but I'm glad I did. If I hadn't hidden it, I would have to go home to get it.

The fleece throw I covered Maddy with that night is hanging over the back of a dining room chair. I wrap myself in it while I feed the cats, who act like it's been days since they saw any food. Rufus complains the loudest. I put a dish out for the dog, and feed Otis and Rav on my way home. I wait to hear Stan's chainsaw in the distance before I cross the yard to my house.

Cindee's in the kitchen, sitting on a stool watching *Let's Make a Deal*. "Door 3!" she shouts at the TV. "Door 3!" She slaps the countertop in frustration when the woman dressed like a chicken chooses Door 1.

I tiptoe across to my room to get dressed. I'm still chilled and look through the closet for a warmer sweater. I spot extra blankets on the top shelf. I pull them down, clear a space on the floor, and shut the louvered door. I wrap myself in one of the blankets and lie down with my head on the second one. They won't think to look for me here.

III

I wake confused about where I am until the sound of the TV in the kitchen orients me. I listen for voices. Cindee's humming to herself instead of chattering like she does if Stan's in the room. I open the louvered door and crawl out of the closet.

I tiptoe down the hall and peek around the corner. Cindee's at the sink peeling and slicing apples for what she calls her "world-famous" applesauce. It's okay, but Mom's was better.

By the time she hears the hinges on the front door creak and calls to me, I'm outside. I dart into the shed before she reaches the porch. Through the grimy shed window, I watch her shade her eyes, shrug, and go back into the house.

I lift my bike off the hook in one of the beams and use a hand pump to put air in the tires. It's a boy's bike Dad bought for my seventh birthday. I don't think I've ridden it since he left. Now I'm so tall, I look like a frog on a lily pad riding it, legs splayed. I'm going to use it anyway to ride out to the end of McDowell Creek Drive to see where the dog comes from.

A mile or so past Maddy's, I reach where the pavement ends but the road doesn't. A half dozen dirt tracks disappear into the woods in all directions, like spokes of a wheel. The two houses nearest where the paved road ends have rusty trucks in the yard with blackberry vines growing out of broken windows and outbuildings with sagging roofs. The only sign one of them is still lived in is a dog chained to a tree. It snarls and barks at me.

I park my bike in a patch of huckleberries and sit out of sight on a downed tree. From here, I can see all the tracks.

About twenty minutes have passed when the chained dog barks again. The sound startles me and I jump. I didn't see Maddy's stray come out of any of the dirt roads, but there he is, almost opposite where I'm hiding, trotting purposefully.

I wait until he's almost out of sight before I start to follow. Part of me wants him to see me, wants him to know he's been caught, though, of course, he hasn't been, since I don't know which road he came down.

I ride home slowly, and don't spot the dog again until I'm at the top of the hill above Maddy's. He's sitting by the mailbox in that sphinxlike pose of his, front paws together, head up, staring at her house.

My bike brakes squeal when I come down the hill. The dog sees me and leaps up. He flattens his ears, wedges his tail between his hind legs, runs across the road, and disappears down the same deer trail I used.

"I'm trying to be your friend!" I shout.

I wait for a couple minutes, hoping he'll come back. He doesn't.

I turn into Maddy's driveway and roll to the bottom. I lean my bike against the front deck railing, get the key, and go in to feed the cats.

CHAPTER 11

I

At dinner that night, I come to the table wearing Mom's white Big River Run baseball cap. She wore it during her last remission. We did the 5K walk together in support of the cancer center. I know Stan recognizes it. He did the 10K run and came in fourth. I stare at him while I chew. He doesn't look at me. Even Cindee's quiet. We eat in silence, then I go to my room.

On Tuesday, I tell Sherri that I have an errand after school. Maddy's been moved to Sherwood Oaks, which is only a mile from school. Cindee agrees to pick me up there.

I don't have many memories of my grandfather here at Sherwood Oaks, except the smell of urine, stale bodies, and Clorox, which hits me the minute I'm in the door. A few old men sit in wheelchairs in a nice sunny room to my left. They're watching the news on a big-screen TV. Against the wall opposite the door is a big fish tank containing two huge black fish. Three old women in wheelchairs are lined up in the corridor across from the nurses' station. They watch me come in, and their eyes follow me to the desk.

"May I help you?" a nurse's aide asks.

"I'm looking for Maddy Baxter."

"Patient or employee?"

"Patient."

The nurse runs her finger down a chart. "She's in room 9. Go left."

The doors to all the rooms are open and each has two beds. Maddy's not going to be happy with a roommate, and the place feels very warm. Maddy hates heat. She sleeps with her sliding glass doors wide open even in winter.

Number 9's window faces an ivy-covered wall that makes the room dark. The bed nearest the door is empty, and the curtain between it and the bed by the window is drawn. I peek around it. Some other woman is in it, asleep with her mouth open. Her teeth are in a glass beside the bed. I back out of the room and bump into an old man in a wheelchair. The footrests are up and he's using his feet to walk the chair down the hall.

"I'm sorry," I say.

He has a nice smile but says nothing. The corridor ladies are still watching me as I make my way to the nurses' station again.

"She's not there," I say when the aide looks up.

"She may be in the physical therapy room. Go all the way down this hall, take a left, and it's at the end on the left."

All the old people's eyes follow me, and I'm conscious of how young I am and how powerfully I can move. I feel the warm air against my skin through the holes in my leggings. I feel like a *Star Trek* character beamed down among a discarded race of people.

Near the end of the corridor, I hear a woman crying out for someone to help her. I hurry a little, not that I expect to be the one to help. The corridor is crowded with carts full of medications, nurses and aides moving in and out of rooms. The lady calling for help is across from another nurses' station. She's slumped in what looks like a leather recliner with wheels. When I reach her, the woman grabs my arm.

"Help. Help. I'm through. Pull my pants up."

Pull your pants up! Stan yelled. I grip the edges of my hoodie sleeves so Maddy won't see the finger-shaped bruises on my wrist.

The old lady presses the back of my hand to her cheek. "Help me, please. I'm through. Pull my pants up."

One of the aides stops. "What the matter, Idalene?"

"I'm through. Pull my pants up."

The aide leans her forward to check her backside and pretends to pull her pants up. "There you go, Idie, all set."

I walk away, and the woman begins calling for help again.

Maddy is in the rehabilitation room. She's using a walker with a wooden platform on the left side for her broken arm. Her eyes are closed, and her face scrunches with pain as she takes a step.

"Good, Maddy," the therapist says.

My eyes are drawn to a man in a wheelchair who has somehow gotten behind a chalkboard. All I can see are his legs and the bottom part of the wheelchair. A male nurse in green scrubs is at a table filling out forms. No one seems to pay any attention to the man behind the chalkboard.

Maddy says, "Look who's here. Lisa, this is my neighbor, Finch Delgado."

"Nice to meet you, Finch."

I know I told Sherri to call me Finch, but it still feels odd to be introduced as if that were my real name. "Hi," I say lamely.

"How's it going at home?" Maddy says. She turns to the therapist. "My girl, here, is taking care of the menagerie for me."

"I love animals. What all do you have?" Lisa asks.

"Cats, birds, and a stray dog," Maddy says.

"That's nice. Lots of company."

"Lots of work, right, Finch?" Maddy smiles at me.

"Not too much. How are you doing?"

Maddy's face sags. "Okay, I guess."

"She's doing great," the therapist says. "But this is definitely the end of her chimney-sweeping career. She's not Mary Poppins."

"How long do you have to stay here?"

"Two weeks," Maddy says, at the same moment the therapist says three.

Lisa smiles. "Maybe two, if she works hard. We don't want to rush things. How about taking a break, and you two can visit." She rolls one of those recliners with wheels over and helps Maddy sit down. "I'll be back. Don't make a break for it."

"If I could run, I would."

When the therapist leaves, I give Maddy a hug and take a chair opposite her. "This seems like a nice place. Do you like it okay?"

"The people who work here are lovely, but if this is a peek at my future, I'd sooner jump off the Noyo Bridge."

"It is kind of sad."

"For you. You're seeing it through the wrong end of a telescope."

"What does that mean?"

"Have you ever looked through the wrong end of a tele-scope or binoculars?"

"Yeah."

"And what did you see?"

"Things look farther away."

"Exactly. But for me I'm seeing it through the right end—large and looming."

The man behind the chalkboard hasn't moved a mus-cle. "What's that man doing back there?" I point.

Maddy glances at my arm before following my gaze. She laughs and flinches. "That's a dummy. They use him for training the aides."

I giggle. "I thought he'd just wheeled back there and been forgotten."

She catches my hand and pushes my sleeve up. "How'd you get those bruises?"

I pull my sleeve down. "Backpack strap."

Maddy squints at me. "Everything okay at home?"

I shrug. "Yeah."

She takes my chin and makes me look at her. "Finch—"

"Time's up, ladies." Lisa's back.

Maddy pats my cheek. "I forgot to ask about the dog."

"He's there twice a day. I go down to feed everybody after school and he's coming from the other end of the road. I rode my bike out to try to find where he lives but missed where he came from."

"I didn't know you had a bike."

"I never ride it. It's the one Dad gave me." She'll remem-ber it's a boy's bike. I'd taken it down to show her, crying because it wasn't the girl's bike I'd wanted.

She nods. "I'd forgotten."

"Need to get back to work, Maddy." Lisa brings her walker over.

I stand. "Guess I better get going. Cindee's picking me up."

"Thanks for coming by, honey. And thank Cindee." She holds out her good arm.

I lean in to hug her.

"I'm in your corner," she whispers. "Don't forget that."

"I know." I hold tight until Maddy lets me go. Tears fill her eyes. "What's wrong?"

She shakes her head. "Nothing, honey. I just wish I could leave with you, that's all."

This reminds me of how my mother used to hold on to my hand as if every ounce of strength she had left in her body were concentrated in her fingers. I regret all the times I pulled free before she was ready to let go. I stop in Maddy's doorway. "I'll be back in a couple days."

"Finch, I've got a bike you can have. It's in the storeroom. I'm sure it's a rusty mess and the tires are flat. Ask Stan to fix it up for you."

"Thanks, Maddy." I wave, but I walk back the way I came thinking the timing is pretty bad to ask Stan to do anything for me.

11

ow is she?" Cindee waits for me to fasten my seat belt.

"Better."

"That's good." She watches me.

"What?"

"Did you tell Maddy about . . . you know . . . yesterday?"

"No."

"He's sorry."

"He hasn't told *me* he's sorry."

"He will, I'm sure."

Cindee is the slowest driver on the planet. By the time we reach the stop sign at Oak and Harold, we've got four cars behind us. She's looked both ways three times. When the guy behind us honks, Cindee steps on the gas and drives into the path of the car on the right that had given up on us ever moving. Cindee slams on the brakes and so does the other guy. Now we're inches apart in the intersection. The man driving the other car rolls his eyes skyward, then gives Cindee a be-my-guest palm-up pass.

She smiles and nods at him. "I bet he's a Christian."

"And praying you'll get out of his way," I mumble.

Cindee gives me a sharp look.

"Maddy said I could have her old bike."

"That's nice."

"It needs a lot of work."

"Stan can fix it."

"Will he?"

"You can ask." She glances at me. "Or maybe we can make a trade."

She's got the heat blasting in the car, but goose bumps spread up my arm. "What kind of trade?"

"We've got something we want to ask you."

We? This is not going to be good. I can tell. "Like what?"

"I went to see our pastor this morning."

"I'm not going to church."

We've made it to the stop sign at Oak and Franklin. This

time the guy behind us gives Cindee a chance to look both ways, then blasts his horn.

She looks in the rearview mirror, waves, and smiles. "I'm not asking you to, though it might just help you."

"I don't need help." I feel my face get hot.

"I'm not sure we agree on that, but anyway, Pastor Larry told me about a Christian summer camp for kids with—" She stomps on the gas to make the light at Main Street. It turns red as we sail through. "What did he call it?"

"I'm not going." I look in the side-view mirror, hoping to see a cop coming after us.

"Gender identity disorder." She smiles over at me like she answered a hard question on *Jeopardy!*

My stomach churns.

"It can be cured. Pastor Larry showed me an article on-line by a poor man who also thought he was a girl. He had surgery and everything only to discover that he suffered from gender identity disorder. Now he's trying to help other children. It's all right here."

She reaches into her purse and hands me a folded piece of paper. "Larry . . . Pastor Larry printed this out for me to give you. Some of these fit you to a T, sweetie."

Causes of Transgender Disorders
- An unstable, unsafe home environment, real or perceived
- Separation from a parent by death or other events
- Serious illness among the family or child
- Domestic violence in the home
- Neglect, perceived or real
- Sexual, physical, or verbal abuse
- A strong opposition disorder from social norms

The key for parents to helping young transgenders is to work with a professional to identify the cause of the stress the child faces.

She and Stan have decided I'm mental.

"Stan and I only want the best for you, and to see you healthy and happy." Cindee squeezes my hand, and for a moment I let how desperately I want to believe she really cares slow my thinking.

"I'm frightened for you, Morgan. I think God is testing you, and if you keep this I'm-a-girl thing up, you'll suffer eternal damnation."

I jerk my hand away, wad up the paper, and throw it to the floor. "I knew I was a girl long before Momma got sick or my father left. I'm not a freak, and I'm not going to any camp to be *fixed*. Maddy won't let you send me away."

I expect her to say that Maddy's got no say-so, but she doesn't. She doesn't speak for two whole traffic lights, then, just before we turn onto Sequoia, she says, "Maddy's very fragile right now. You wouldn't want to do anything to jeopardize her recovery, would you?"

Of course I wouldn't, but without her I feel powerless and terrified. Can they make me go away? *Summer camp.* It sounds so nontoxic. "Next summer?" I say aloud.

"That's right." There's a hopeful note in her voice.

Halloween is coming up. Summer is months away. Maddy will be fine by then, and I'll have figured out how to find my father.

CHAPTER 12

During the week, while Maddy's still at Sherwood Oaks, I begin to snoop. I don't go through anything personal, but I pay more attention to Maddy's paintings and the things she's collected.

There are faded photos of two children in an album in the bookcase—a boy about seven and a little girl about three. I don't know if Maddy's ever been married. I've never heard her mention any children, so I've assumed all this time she didn't have any. It seems strange to have known Maddy all my life and not know more about her than that she loves animals and likes to paint.

My curiosity grows, as does my comfort level. Maddy's house feels more like home than my own, and it's a shorter walk to the creek to visit my mom. I can see my twin trees from Maddy's back deck and watch the mist rising off the waterfall.

I have a pitiful assortment of keepsakes myself—things I collected after my father left that I keep in my old mermaid backpack on the top shelf of my closet. My favorite is a picture of Mom and Dad dressed for their senior prom at Fort Bragg High School. It's not a professional shot. My grandfather took it, and they're standing by the front door of our house. Because she's wearing heels, my mom is taller than my dad.

Most of the time I hate being tall, but when I look at that picture, I'm proud to be tall like she was.

I have my father's mother-of-pearl penknife, and an expired driver's license with a picture of him as a teenager. He has long hair—the same blondish brown color as mine—a pitiful-looking mustache, and pimples.

I have his Fort Bragg High School class ring on a gold chain, which I found in my mother's jewelry box. I have the nub of a pencil he chewed on, a piece of green glass Dad and I found at Glass Beach, his report card from fifth grade with a warning that he was becoming disruptive in class. I found a spare key to his car in a puddle in the driveway.

These little things he left behind are now my treasures. I like to imagine how surprised he'll be when I find him and he sees all the stuff I've saved. Then I remember what he used to say when he was proud of me: *That's my boy.* He's been away a long time; I bet he's different now. I'll let him get to know me again, then we can talk about it.

Maddy's treasures make me curious about what's important to her. Her paintings seem to have the same thing in common: a way in. Each has a path, a rutted road, or a trail.

Maddy lived in Florida before moving to Northern California. The painting over her mantel behind the woodstove is the largest and one she did when she lived there. It's of pink azaleas blooming beneath a canopy of live oak trees. The path that winds through them looks cool and shady.

My favorite is one of the trails through the redwoods to my spot by the creek. I've never seen Maddy there painting, but it's perfect. I can stare at it and almost feel the cool air the rush of water creates as it comes around a curve in the creek to flow past my twin trees. Maddy even added the worn traces my feet have made crossing the redwood bridge that lies across the creek. The waterfall isn't in the painting, but on the right side of the canvas, mist rises ghostlike, so you know it's there. Even someone who'd never seen it would know it was there.

The painting hangs on the side wall of the breakfast nook. I get a Coke from the fridge and sit opposite it. For the first time, I notice there's a shadowy hint of someone sitting on the cushion of redwood leaves. I get up and go around the table for a closer look. There's the side of a leg with the knee drawn up, and a knobby shoulder. It's me. The part of my head that I can see is crescent-moon-shaped and tilted up.

I feel touched and loved.

II

During the second week of taking care of the house and the animals for Maddy, something in the fridge begins to smell. I, who hate cleaning my own room, decide to clean for Maddy. I start with the refrigerator, which is jammed with the remains of sauces, chutneys, salad dressings, and rotting salad ingredients. I carry these to the compost heap and empty the jars of salsa, pesto, and spaghetti sauce, all green with mold. I rinse the jars and cans and put them in separate bags for recycling.

Maddy doesn't take garbage-pickup service because she recycles nearly everything—even the occasional mouse

Rufus kills. She puts the body on the wall by the compost heap for a raven to find.

By the time I finish, I've filled five paper sacks, four with empty bottles and jars, plastic containers, newspaper flyers, and the junk mail, the fifth with cans and bottles that can be redeemed for cash.

A black bear recently tore up the compost container, and there are the nightly visits by raccoons, skunks, and possums, so I leave the sacks lined up in her living room. The recycling center is north of town and so is one of Cindee's home health clients. I go home to ask if she'd drop them off on her way to work.

Since Stan's not employed, he'd be the obvious one to ask, but he got stopped by the police two days ago for a broken taillight. That's when I found out he's been driving on a suspended license for a DUI he got three weeks ago. He had a week to go to get limited driving privileges back, but he was pulled over by a cop he didn't know. Now he has to go to court and his license could be suspended for six months to a year.

Cindee's standing at the sink, eating a sandwich and watching a soap on TV.

"Maddy's got a big load of recycling. Would you have time to drop it off tomorrow? I separated the cans and bottles." Cindee and Stan save his beer cans to cash in.

"Huh?" She doesn't take her eyes off the screen.

"Maddy's recycling?"

"Oh, sure. Are there any cans?"

I don't say what I'm thinking. "A bag full." I put the mayo and cold cuts back in the fridge and use the sponge to wipe the counter. "You think Stan could load them in the truck?"

"I don't know where he is," Cindee says. "Did you look in the shed?"

"No, but will you ask him?"

"Ask him what?"

I roll my eyes. "Never mind." I can't imagine how anyone can spend so much time in front of the TV. For Christmas last year, Stan increased their Dish service to include a DVR, so now if Cindee has to pee, she stops the action so she doesn't miss a single syllable.

Stan is leaving the shed as I come out of the front door. The wheelbarrow he's pushing is loaded with a couple of chainsaws and a pile of ropes. He kicks the shed door closed with his heel, crosses the yard, and turns down the trail into the state park. Instead of calling to him, I stay hidden behind the screen door until he disappears, then follow him, making sure to stay far enough behind so he won't hear me.

The last time I took this trail was with my mom looking for mushrooms. Both sides are still thick with huckleberries, manzanita, Labrador tea, and rhododendrons, but where the trail starts to slope down toward the creek used to be nearly impassable with fallen trees and limbs. It's now as manicured as a park. The limbs are gone and all the downed trees have been cut up. I knew that was what he'd been doing, but the amount he's removed blows my mind. In the space between towering pairs of Doug firs, the wood is neatly stacked in rows as long as I am tall.

The North Coast of California is always chilly. The winters are rainy and cold, and in summer, fog can blanket the coast from June through September. The only heat in our house is a wood-burning stove, and it goes day and night during the winter and on foggy days in the summer.

Mom used to order two cords of wood a year, but Cindee likes the house warmer, so we use more.

I follow the sound of the squeaky wheel, stop when I hear it stop, then tiptoe forward, watching the trail so I don't step on a twig. I hesitate near a tall rhododendron. I can't see him and don't hear anything for a minute or two. Keeping low, I creep forward, stopping when I hear the snap of a metal ring. I hear him grunt, and watch a weighted line sail up and over one of the lower limbs of a redwood.

Very little sun used to get through the canopy, but now the path is open and sunny. I look up. Dozens of the trees have been limbed as high as thirty or forty feet off the ground. They look like Q-tips—straight, limbless trunks with dense growth at the top.

Stan, wearing a hard hat and goggles, is attaching one end of the rope he tossed over the limb to the belt he's wearing. The belt circles his waist and has two more leather bands, one around each thigh. Over his work boots are braces. Each has a long, sharp spike that extends past his instep. One of the chainsaws dangles from a long length of rope that is attached to his belt.

I watch him ring the trunk of the tree with a second rope, tighten the one he threw over the limb, and lean back. Supporting himself with the rope draped around the trunk, he drives one spiked boot into the trunk and then the other. He flips the rope a few feet up the trunk, climbs after it, then flips it again, tightening the safety rope as he ascends.

He's about twenty feet up the trunk when he reaches the lowest limb. He detaches the chainsaw from his belt and pulls the starter cord. The chainsaw screams as it cuts through. Wood chips and sawdust rain down. There's a loud crack before the limb crashes to the ground.

He takes his finger off the chainsaw's trigger, and it dies.

"Why are you doing that?" I say.

Stan's right foot slips. He swings sideways, is dashed against the tree trunk, bounces a bit, then dangles and swings like a pendulum from the safety rope. "Jesus. You scared the hell out of me."

"What are you doing?"

"Making sure we have enough firewood to last us awhile."

"You know it's illegal, right?"

"I can't afford to care, Morgan. It's the best thing for the forest, and for us. We don't have the money to buy the wood we need, and there was so much just rotting away here, if we had a forest fire, there'd be no stopping it."

It's not the best thing for the forest, but I don't argue. All sorts of animals make their homes in dead trees and downed limbs. "What if a ranger comes? They'll know you did this."

"I doubt anyone in Parks remembers they own this piece of land."

"Where'd you learn to climb trees like that? It looks dangerous."

"I taught myself, and it's only dangerous if someone sneaks up on you." He looks down at me. "What are you doing here, anyway?"

I shrug. "I came to ask you to load Maddy's recycling in the truck. Cindee'll take them to the center tomorrow."

"How about a trade? I could use some help here."

"Like what?"

"You can stack the limbs and use the small chainsaw to cut them up for kindling."

"I don't know how to use a chainsaw." Mom never let me use ours even when I asked to help. I don't say this to Stan.

"'Bout time you learned, then."

"I'll stack the limbs."

A smirky look crosses Stan's face before he pulls the saw cord and the blade screams through the next branch.

I drag limbs into the clearing and stack them until Stan finishes with the tree he's in and rappels down. He looks at the neat pile I've made. "Nice job." He takes off his gear and loads it into the wheelbarrow. "I'm going in for lunch. Coming?"

"I had a big breakfast."

"Suit yourself."

III

I don't follow him. I cut straight down to the creek, weaving through the redwoods and dense ferns. I come out on a trail that runs parallel to the flow of water. It will take me back to Maddy's.

I'm watching where I'm walking and am almost to Maddy's when I look up. The dog sits at the top of the incline. I don't stop climbing, so he gets up and runs a few yards, and turns to look back at me.

"You're an idiot," I say. "I'm the one feeding you, you know."

The dog hides behind a tree in the yard, but both his head and rear end show.

I throw up my arms. "Boo."

He shoots across the yard, tail between his legs, and races up the hill to the road.

"Dog, stop. I'm sorry."

But he doesn't stop or even look back.

What's wrong with me, scaring that poor dog? I need a friend as much as he does.

IV

Stan drags in shortly before dinner. "Hi, honey," Cindee says. "Do you want a beer before you get cleaned up?" She stands on tiptoes to kiss his cheek.

He's stripped down to his sweat-stained undershirt, and the sides of his jeans are filthy from wiping his hands on them.

"You're wrong, you know," I say. I'm sitting on a kitchen stool, watching *Jeopardy!*

"About what?"

"Cleaning up fallen trees is not good for the forest." I turn back to the TV.

"Are you our resident botanist now?"

"I'm just telling you," I say without looking at him. "All sorts of things live under logs, and in them. You can ask Maddy if you don't believe me."

"Our needs trump a slug's."

"Salamanders lay their eggs in rotting logs." I still don't look at him.

"Enough." Stan slaps the table. "Why aren't you helping Cindee with dinner?"

"I offered."

"Yes, he did, honey."

"Well, how about setting the table?"

"Right after final *Jeopardy!*"

Stan walks over, picks up the remote, and turns off the TV. "I think we need some new rules and duties around here. Cindee is not your slave."

"I never said she was."

"Then get off your butt and set the table."

I bite my lip. "You're not the boss of me."

"We're adults, you're a kid. That gives us the final say."

"It's my house." I pick up the remote and turn the TV back on, but flinch when Stan snatches it out of my hand and turns it off. "Turn it on again and I'll kick the screen in."

"Honey. Sweetie," Cindee coos.

"Stay out of this," he snaps. "He's either down at that old lady's house or lazing around by the creek. He needs to be doing some of the work around here. His room's a mess, but he'll clean up that old lady's without batting an eye."

My heart pounds. I'm mad and scared. I glance at Cindee.

She shrugs and opens the fridge.

I want to tell them to get out of my house, but I'm a minor. The county could put me in foster care unless I can find my father and make Stan and Cindee leave. For all I know, Stan probably has official custody of me. I get up and take plates from the cupboard.

V

Since I shouted at him, the dog is more cautious. He doesn't wait at the end of the trail for me as he'd started doing and stays up by the road until I leave. I buy him a can of wet food and put out half of it with his dry food, hoping he'll know I'm sorry for yelling at him.

On Saturday, I try to find his home again. I leave Maddy's at about three thirty and ride all the way to where the pavement ends. The shell of an abandoned car is rusting in the weeds at the side of the road. It's been gutted, and all the windows are broken out. Everything that could be stolen from it has been, including the seats and the rearview mirror. Unless the dog comes from the dirt track directly behind me, the car will give me cover. I roll my bike into the bushes, and squat beside the rear bumper to wait.

I've been crouched so long, my calf muscles are cramping, and I am about to give up when I spot him. He's coming out of a road about a hundred feet from where I'm hiding. I hold my breath. If he glances this way, he'll see me. When he's out of sight, I get my bike, and walk it to the bottom of the long, rutted, steep uphill driveway. There's no mailbox, no street number, and I can't see what's beyond the crest.

I stand for a while trying to decide whether to go up for a look. This whole end of the road creeps me out with its abandoned cars, chained dogs, and weed-choked yards.

The sound of a car coming finally makes me move. I jump on my bike and, pedaling hard, start up the hill. I'm about a quarter of the way when the car zooms by, cuts sharply left, and drives up one of the dirt tracks on the other side of the road.

I dismount and push my bike the rest of the way. As I near the top, I go more slowly. I don't want to surprise anyone, and I don't want to be surprised myself.

At first, I think this must be a trash dump, like places I've come across in the woods before. Instead of taking their stuff to the Caspar refuse center, where they have to pay, people drive into the forest to dump their junk—washing machines, old cars, mattresses, bottles and cans. But this looks like someone used to live here. There's a tire hanging from a rope tied to a tree limb, and a sand-filled tractor tire with an armless doll buried to its neck.

This isn't one pile of trash; it looks like scattered leftovers from a family's life. Weeds grow around scorched circles where brush has been burned. There are empty wire cages. From the pile of droppings beneath them, one was a rabbit hutch and the other a chicken coop. A rotting hammock stretches between two spindly cypress trees. Weeds have taken over, except for a rectangle of bare ground with four concrete blocks, one at each corner. A trailer had been there, and it hasn't been gone long enough for weeds to fill the space it left.

Whoever lived here took the trailer but left the steps to the front door behind—the steps and the dog.

I wonder how long the dog waited before he went looking for someone with a heart big enough to put food out for him. A week? Two? Maddy said he was skin and bones when he first showed up. I kick the charred remains of a couple of beer cans.

"He loved you!" I shout. "How could you leave him behind?"

A bit of red fabric catches my eye in one of the scorched circles. I find a stick and scratch at it. It's a burned dog collar. His owners took his collar off and threw it in the fire. All that's left is a one-inch piece with two letters: *B-E*. I can't tell if they are the first two letters, the last two, or something in between.

Every day, twice a day, he comes to Maddy's to be fed, then walks the mile and a half home to wait for his family to come back for him. I wipe as much of the dirt off as I can and put the collar in my pocket.

CHAPTER 13

I

The weather is balmy for late October. Sherri and I carry our lunch trays to a picnic table in the courtyard. I'm curious about how her mother manages to meet so many men. I've just asked her when I hear Amanda shriek with laughter. She's sitting a few tables away and has been giggling, laughing, and flipping her hair like this is the most fun she's ever had eating cafeteria food.

"Online," Sherri says.

I look over when Amanda shrieks. Gabe is crossing the courtyard with a couple of his friends. As hard as she's trying, he doesn't even glance in her direction.

There's a momentary delay before what Sherri said sinks in. "What did you say?"

"She meets them on places like Match.com and eHarmony."

Chill bumps spread up my arms. I've never had any real idea about how to find my father. I can't imagine why it never occurred to me to search online.

I don't have a computer of my own, so I wait until Cindee and Stan leave on their once-a-week date night to use

Cindee's. The thought of how easy it might be to find him makes my hands shake as I type his name into Google. One Morgan Delgado comes up with a link to Facebook. I follow that link and find five: four women and a young boy. I try a site called Addresses.com, where I type in my own address. The lump in my throat feels like it will choke me when Mom's name comes up.

When my father left, he said he was going to Oregon to look for work. I type "Oregon" into the blank for State. Zero. When I delete the state, nine Morgan Delgados come up— none in Oregon; one in Colorado; three in California. The rest are in the East.

There's a suggestion at the bottom of the page to try "M. Delgado." I put in the initial and "Oregon" again. Twelve names come up, but I can't be sure the *M* stands for Morgan. I try to narrow it down by previous cities but none lists Fort Bragg. On the far right side of the page is a list of relatives, but neither my name nor my mother's appears. What if he moved on from Oregon? He could be anywhere.

II

The best memory I have of my father is from when I was seven and a half. Mom had just been diagnosed with breast cancer for the second time. We had fog every day for weeks, and Mom said she needed to feel sun on her face, so Dad drove us inland. Our Ford Explorer had a digital thermometer reading of the outside temperature. I became fascinated watching it rise and called out every time it went up a degree. It was fifty-eight degrees when we left the coast. By the time we reached Willits, thirty-three miles away, it was ninety-nine.

"Where to?" Dad asked. We'd stopped for chocolate milkshakes at Burger King.

"I don't care." Mom pushed the button to open the moon-roof, put her head back, and closed her eyes. "Laytonville. Let's drive up to Laytonville. My parents used to take me there once every summer to a motel with a swimming pool." She leaned around to look at me. "Would you like to go swimming?"

"Yes!" I clapped my hands together. "But I didn't bring my bathing suit."

"Who cares? You can swim in your underwear."

"Yeah. Let's go to Lakenville."

My parents laughed. "They should change the town's name to Lakenville," Mom said.

"Do you remember how to swim?" Dad's eyes smiled at me in the rearview mirror.

I put my head down, cupped my hands, and swung my arms like the swim instructor at the rec center pool taught me. That pool was enclosed, heated, and reeked of chlorine. I'd never been in an outdoor pool.

There wasn't much to the town of Laytonville: a hardware store, a restaurant, a gas station, a realty office, and three motels. "It was the Cottage Motel." My mother pointed.

Since the pool was for guests only, Dad got us a room. I jumped on the bed while Mom collected towels for us to use.

There was no one in the pool—a good thing, since Dad went in in his plaid boxer shorts, and I in my underpants. This was before Mom started buying me girls' panties, or

Dad would have turned us around and driven us home. Mom lay in a deck chair and fell asleep.

I remember calling "Watch me!" to Dad every time I cannonballed off the diving board into the water. I remember him putting a finger to his lips so my shouts wouldn't wake Mom. I'd whispered "watch me" after that.

I type his name into the computer again, scroll to the bottom, and click on USSearch.com. While the page loads, my mind goes back to the motel pool. My father reached his hand out, which I took, and I let myself be reeled into a new game. He'd pull me in, pick me up, then toss me backward into the water. I loved the momentary sensation of flying, but it was his callused hand reaching for me again and again that now gives me the hope that, if I find him, he will still want me.

There are dozens of Morgan Delgados listed on the US Search page. I get up and go to my closet for my backpack full of keepsakes. I find my dad's fifth-grade report card, but there's no middle initial. At the bottom of the box is his old driver's license. His middle name is Anthony. Morgan A. Delgado. I go back to the computer and type in his full name.

None of the Morgan A. Delgados live in Oregon, but there are three in California, the closest in Eureka, which is a three-hour drive north of Fort Bragg.

My mother would be thirty-five. One M. Delgado is fifty-nine. I eliminate him—if he is a him. The other two are thirty-six and thirty-eight. Neither Mom nor I are listed as relatives, and Fort Bragg isn't on the list of places either has lived. I look at Dad's driver's license and do the math. He's thirty-seven. Chill bumps spread up my arms. If the website is out of date, the one who's thirty-six could be my dad. I click on "View Details." A new page comes up, and you have to pay to go further. I can get an address and phone number for ninety-five cents, but I need a credit card.

Now what?

CHAPTER 14

After the first time I hopped off the school bus to ride with Deanne and Sherri, the driver said no when I tried it the next day. Amanda let out a loud "ha" when the driver told me to sit back down. I haven't ridden the bus since.

Stan never apologized, but he did fix up Maddy's old bike. He bought new tires and a new chain, cleaned off the rust, and sprayed it with WD-40. I thought he did it for me as a way of showing he *was* sorry, but he's been using it to ride down to the end of Sequoia to the Mobil station for beer.

The next time he was in the woods cutting down trees, I moved it to Maddy's pump house, which has a padlock. He didn't even ask.

Now, in the mornings, I go to feed the animals, wheel it out to the road, and wait until the bus goes by before riding it to Sherri's house, which is all downhill. The bus makes so many stops along the way, I usually beat it to their house. I leave my bike chained to a tree and ride it home again in the afternoons.

11

Sherri wants to go to Wall Street for Halloween. I've never been but know it's where hundreds of kids gather and go house to house trick-or-treating. "We have to wear costumes," she says.

"I don't have anything."

"Make something out of a sheet, like a toga. Or get your mom to order something sent over from Walmart."

"Okay," I say instead of, *Slim chance*. I haven't told Sherri I live with my stepparents, or that my father left us and my mother is dead. I didn't want her feeling sorry for me. And, of course, I want to stay friends so I haven't told her that I was born a boy.

There's a sheet in the linen closet that I could make a toga out of. Cindee washed it with her bathrobe, which turned it pink. I practice wrapping it and tying it, but don't like how dumb it looks.

A couple days later, I come out of my room and hear Stan and Cindee in the kitchen.

"Get it, if you want it," Stan says.

"It's hand-forged wrought iron."

The door to their bedroom is standing open and from the hallway, I see the eBay logo on the computer screen. "Metal Art Cross," it says, with a picture of a big black curly cross.

"It's $29.99 if I use 'Buy It Now,' and the shipping's free."

"How many days till the auction ends?"

"Eighteen."

"Get it now."

"Yippee! I love you." She hugs him.

Cindee's purse, as usual, is on one of the kitchen counter stools. She opens it, takes out her wallet, and pulls out a credit card. She waves it in the air. "You're sure?"

"I'm sure," Stan says.

The floor creaks as Cindee crosses the living room. I duck back into my room and close the door, leaving a crack for me to peek through.

Just as Cindee sits down at the computer, Stan calls, "Hey, babe. Do we have any of that pumpkin pancake mix left?"

"Lots. Want me to make pancakes?"

"I can do it."

I see Cindee smile to herself, push back in the chair, and get up. "I'll do it, sweetie." She comes out into the hall. "Morgan, you want pumpkin pancakes?"

On my tiptoes, I dash to the far side of my room. "What?" I call as if I'm too far away to hear.

"You want pumpkin pancakes?" Cindee says, louder this time.

"No, thanks." Why can't she remember I hate the taste of pumpkin?

I wait by my door until I hear their low lovey-dovey voices in the kitchen. "Stop that." Cindee giggles. "What if Morgan comes in?"

I pad down the hall into their room. Cindee's credit card is beside the mouse. I tear off a yellow Post-it Note and copy down the number, Cindee's full name, the expiration date, and the three-digit code on the back.

III

Stan's gone to limb more trees. Cindee's in the shower. She takes forever in the bathroom, so I know I've got time to use her computer to order a Halloween costume from Walmart. I find a mermaid one, order it with Cindee's credit card, and have it sent to Maddy's. Cindee's always ordering stuff online. I doubt she'll even notice.

I hear water stop in the shower and the swish of the curtain. She still has to dry her hair, use hot rollers, and put on a pound of makeup. I quickly find the US Search site again, pay the ninety-five cents for one-time access, and get the three M. Delgado numbers.

Cindee is singing to herself in the bathroom, so I dial the first number on list.

"Hola," the voice on the other end says in Spanish. "¿Juan?" The woman asks.

I find my voice. It trembles. "My name is Morgan Delgado."

"Is this a solicitation?" she asks in perfect English. "We're on the Do Not Call list."

"No, ma'am. My name *is* Morgan Delgado. I'm named after my father, and I'm trying to find him. Is there a Morgan Delgado living there?"

"I'm Maria Delgado. No Morgan."

"Oh."

"I have another call coming in. What's your number? I'll call you back."

I can't have this person call here. Cindee might answer. "Never mind." I hang up.

Five seconds later, the phone rings. "Hello?"

"Don't call here again," the voice says.

I'd forgotten about *69. "You're not the right person, so why would I?"

After that, I decide to go to Maddy's to make the next call.

Cindee comes out of the bathroom, toweling her hair. "Who was on the phone?"

"A wrong number. I'm going down to Maddy's."

"Isn't it too early to feed the animals?"

"I'm going to vacuum and change her sheets. She's coming home next Wednesday."

"Am I supposed to pick her up?"

"Can we?"

Cindee shrugs. "Sure. I'll DVR my programs."

I turn to go before rolling my eyes.

CHAPTER 15

Last time I visited her at Sherwood Oaks, I brought
Maddy her cell phone. After I feed the critters, I call
her to check in. "Hi, Maddy."

"Hi, Finch. Is everything okay?"

"Everything is fine. I came down to clean the house for
you before you come home."

"You don't have to do that. A friend has a housekeeper
she likes. I'll see if she's available."

"I don't mind." Then another thought occurs to me. "How
much do you pay?"

"Why?"

"Could I clean your house in trade for letting me use
your phone for a couple long-distance calls?"

"The going rate for housekeepers is twenty an hour. Are
you calling Europe?"

"Eureka."

There is silence for a minute. "Finch, are you trying to
find your father?"

"Yes."

Silence again. "I'm not sure that's a good idea."

I'm sitting at Maddy's desk watching the chipmunks in her bird feeder. Sunlight slants through the Venetian blinds, casting bars of light on the wall and me.

"Finch?"

I take a breath. "How come?"

"I just don't want to see you hurt."

"He might have lost track of me."

"Count your blessings."

"What does that mean?" I feel defensive.

"Nothing. I shouldn't have said it. Of course you can use my phone. Just prepare yourself, okay? He's been gone a long time. People move on."

A man answers my next call. "Yeah?"

I realize that I don't remember my father's voice. This could be him. "Does Morgan Delgado live there?"

"Who wants to know?"

"I'm . . ." Maddy's warning comes to mind: *prepare your-self*. "I'm trying to locate Morgan Delgado. My father."

There's a short laugh on the other end. "I got no kids— that I know of. Who's your mother?" He laughs again.

I hang up and wait for the phone to ring. It doesn't.

The entire wall to my right is lined with books, floor to ceiling. I get up and begin to read the titles and authors off some of the spines: *The Viking Portable Library: Mark Twain*, Steinbeck, Dickens, *The Complete Sherlock Holmes*, *The Complete Works of Shakespeare*, and a bunch of books by Barbara Kingsolver.

I step closer, put my finger against one of the titles, close my eyes, and wish I could absorb all the knowledge of these authors. I want to understand everything: why my mother died, why my father left, why God—if there is a god—made me the way I am. What makes people cruel, or kind? How you know when a friendship is real—or not. How love works; how long grief lasts.

I open my eyes. The dog is on the front deck watching me through the sliding glass door. He's as close as he's ever come—but still safely behind a wall of glass. "I'm as stupid about life as you are." I put my hand flat against the cold pane.

The dog's tail wags once and stops. He's as full of doubts as I am.

There's only one M. Delgado left who's the right age. I dial the number. It rings six times before a machine answers. I don't want to leave a message and am about to hang up when I hear "Hello" over the recorded message. "Hang on," the woman says.

The message to leave your number and the time and day you called ends. "Hello," the woman says again.

"Yes, ma'am. My name . . . I'm trying to reach Morgan Delgado."

"I'm sorry. There's no one here by that name. We have a Martin and a Mike, but no Morgan." Her voice is nice, like she's smiling.

"Okay. I'm sorry to have bothered you."

"No bother. Hope you find him . . ." She laughs. "Or her. Can't tell nowadays, can you?"

I shake my head. "I guess not."

"Good luck."

"Thank you."

To realize that the woman who was mean and the man

who was nasty were not who I'm looking for is a relief, but the woman who was nice was my last chance—the final M. Delgado on the website.

I put my head on my arm and cry.

CHAPTER 16

I

When I go down to feed the animals after school on Friday, the package with the mermaid costume I ordered from Walmart and had sent to Maddy's address is leaning against her front door.

The costume is short on me but baggy enough to hide what needs to be hidden. I don't even like mermaids anymore, not like I did when I was little and thought having a fish tail beat having a penis. Sadly, I look almost as dumb in it as I looked wrapped in a pink sheet but it's too late now. Sherri and Deanne are picking me up at six.

I tell Cindee I'm spending the night at Maddy's to guard the house. We never get any trick-or-treaters, and neither does Maddy. Cindee believes me because she and Stan don't care. They probably wish I'd move down there. I wish I could, too.

Deanne's got a date and drops us off as close to Wall Street as she can get in the traffic. Walking in the mermaid costume isn't easy. My light blue Converse All Stars match the costume but the skirt is so narrow at the bottom I have to walk like a duck. Sherri's wearing a toga she made out of an old sheet. She has curves and boobs so it would look good if she didn't have to wear a coat over it. It's a cold night and threatening to rain.

We go house to house, trailing behind cute little kids, collecting candy. I feel stupid and too old to be doing this, and I'm freezing. I didn't think to bring a coat, and the light blue sweater I'm wearing is one of Maddy's.

"Morgan?"

I recognize the voice but keep walking. I'd run if I could. It's Sherri who stops and turns. My heart begins to thunder.

"Hey, Morgan. Is that you? It's Sammy."

Sammy was my best friend in first and second grade—back before my father left and I let my hair grow, before I started Dana Gray Elementary as a girl instead of boy. I turn.

He's dressed in a red-and-gold Quidditch robe and looking at me with his head cocked to one side, mystified.

"Hi, Sammy. What are you doing here?" He's with another kid I've never seen before.

"Visiting my grandparents. This is my cousin, Jacob. Why are you dressed like a girl?"

I glance at Sherri, my first real friend since Sammy moved away. She's staring at me, eyebrows drawn down in a V. I swallow the feeling that I might throw up and take a deep breath. "Because I *am* a girl."

"No, you're not." He looks at Jacob. "No, he's not."

"Yes, I am."

Sammy glances at my crotch. I suppose he can't help himself. "You were a boy."

Two kids run by screaming, followed by a white sheet with eyeholes.

Sherri's either my friend or she's not. There's nothing I can do but hope. I feel myself on the verge of smiling at the picture of Sherri dumping me right here and now and me walking five miles home in this dumb costume. "How do you know you're a boy, Sammy?"

"That's stupid. Because I know."

"That's exactly how I feel. I have a boy's body, but in here"—I tap my fish-scale-covered heart—"I'm a girl." I glance at Sherri.

"Oh my God," Sammy says, "you've turned into a homo."

"No, she's not," Sherri says. "She's transgender, which has nothing to do with which sex she will be attracted to."

I close my eyes and swallow my joy.

"Come on, Finch. My sister's waiting for us." Sherri takes my hand and tugs me past Sammy and Jacob, who fall into each other's arms laughing.

||

We arranged to meet Deanne at the Headlands Coffeehouse, a place where other kids her age hang out. It's about a mile. With me walking in tiny little steps, it takes us about thirty minutes. I can't wait to burn this costume in Maddy's woodstove.

For a block or two, I don't know what to say. Maybe Sherri doesn't, either. We walk side by side, hugging ourselves against the cold.

I'm the first to speak. "I'm sorry I didn't tell you. Do you hate me?"

"Of course not. Besides, I kind of guessed it two weeks ago."

I stop short and have to swing my arms not to lose my balance. "You did?"

"When we went to the Starr Center for Lauren's birthday party. You wore that bathing suit with the dorky skirt. Who'd wear that unless they had to? And if you remember, the water there is pretty cold." She smiles at me.

Lauren had insisted I come to her party and invited Sherri since she knew we'd become friends. "I hate that suit. It's two years old and it took all my nerve to wear it."

"I sure hope so."

We both laugh, then I'm suddenly crying.

Sherri puts her arm around me. "What's the matter?"

I shake my head.

"Come on. It's no big deal. I lived in Vegas, remember?"

"My stepparents think I've got a mental disorder because my mother died and my father left us."

"Jeez. You're living with stepparents. That's bad."

"They want to send me to some Jesus camp this summer where they treat kids like me."

"That neighbor of yours won't let that happen, right?"

"I don't know whether she can stop them. I've been looking for my real father."

"Where is he?"

"Oregon, I think. Last I heard, anyway. I thought I might have found him in Eureka, but the number I called wasn't him."

We cut down an alley, which blocks the wind a little.

"What are you going to do when your voice starts to change?"

"I don't know, but it's practically all I think about."

"I knew this kid at my last school. He was trans—born

a girl. He took hormones or something to keep from getting boobs."

I'm haunted by the thought of my voice changing and having to shave. Worse is knowing Cindee and Stan will never let me take anything to stop it from happening.

We enter the Headlands Coffeehouse through the back door. Deanne's leaning against the bike rack outside the front door. Some guy has his arm around her shoulders. She doesn't look all that happy to see us—a mermaid and her toga-wearing little sister.

I get in line to order some tea. Sherri wants a milkshake. "You know what? If you find your dad, I bet my sister would drive you up to meet him."

"Why would she do that?"

Sherri shrugs. "We both like being anywhere but home."

CHAPTER 17

It's Sunday evening, and I'm sitting in Maddy's recliner watching the episode of *Supergirl* I recorded. Rufus is on my lap, snoring. When Cory and Risty run to the window, he suddenly sits up and stares into the blackness, too.

This always makes me nervous even though it usually turns out to be a skunk or a raccoon, but a couple months ago, Maddy had a pair of mountain lions walk past her front window.

I pause the DVR and listen. There's no sound, but the cats are still on high alert. If it were the dog, the cats would have hidden. I get up, turn on the front porch light, and part the Venetian blinds. It's a baby possum about the size of a big rat, and it's sniffing around under the suet feeder.

I'm reaching to turn the light out when I notice there's something odd about the way it's walking. I raise the blinds and squat down to look at its feet. They're covered in pine needles, so thickly it looks like it's wearing boots. I go to the kitchen and grab a dish towel. Once outside, I tiptoe around to the front deck. It doesn't seem to hear, see, or smell me.

I listen to its breathing, which sounds a little like Rufus when he snores. Maybe it's sick, except that wouldn't explain the pine needles. Then I have an aha moment. I've stepped on enough banana slugs to know what happened. Slugs secrete a slime that can stick your fingers together. Once it's on you, everything you step on sticks to the bottom of your shoe.

The possum is too small to have squished a slug, so it must have tried to eat it. Maddy says lots of animals eat banana slugs.

The baby continues to thump around under the feeder on its pine-needle feet. The birds haven't left much in the way of missed bits of suet, but there's a greasy slick on the wooden deck. The possum turns its head sideways like it's trying to lick the spot. That seems odd. It then tries to wipe its mouth on the wood, first one side then the other, then claws at its mouth.

I know possums have needle-sharp teeth, so I'm careful. I stay still and wait for it to wander within range, then using the dish towel, I grab the baby right behind its head and around the middle with my other hand. It kicks once, then goes limp, playing dead. I hold it up to the porch light. Not only is its mouth glued shut with slug goop, one nostril is plugged. That's why its breathing sounds ragged.

I carry the baby possum into the house and run water in the sink until it turns warm. It's still playing dead, its eyes closed, head lolled to one side, little sides heaving. I take a tiny front paw and hold it under the stream of warm water. The slime gets slimier and begins to foam. I put a bit of dish soap on it, but that makes it worse.

Good thing I didn't start with its nose. If the other nostril gets plugged, the baby will suffocate. I glance at the clock on the oven. It's nine thirty. Too late to call Maddy. I look under the sink for something else that might work. There's nothing that doesn't sound toxic: Comet, Soft Scrub, OxiClean. I look at the clock again. Two minutes have passed. I have to call her.

I wrap the dish towel around the possum, leaving just its nose exposed, and lay it in the sink. I run to Maddy's office to look for the piece of paper I wrote her cell phone number on and take the phone back to the kitchen. The baby's worked itself free of the dish towel and is walking around in the sink. I start to dial but hang up before it rings. She probably turns her phone off at night, and if she didn't it will wake her, and her roommate. I get the phone book and look up the number for Sherwood Oaks.

"I need to talk to Maddy Baxter," I say when a woman answers.

"I'm sure she's asleep by now."

"This is an emergency. I have to talk to her."

"Well, let me go see if she's awake."

She must be carrying the phone because I hear the woman's shoes squeak as she walks down the hall to Maddy's room.

"Mrs. Baxter," she whispers.

Someone's snoring.

"She's asleep," the woman says.

"You have to wake her."

"What exactly is your emergency?" She sounds suspicious.

"It's . . . it's an animal emergency. One of her animals. I need her to tell me what to do."

"Mrs. Baxter. Mrs. Baxter."

The snoring stops, and there is whispering.

"Finch? What's wrong?"

"Maddy, I've got a baby possum that tried to eat a banana slug. Its mouth is sealed shut and so is one nostril. What do I do?"

"Well, don't use water. That will only make it worse. Use dry paper towels and, Finch, you are going to have to clean its mouth out. Can you do that?"

"I'll try, but how? Won't it bite me?"

"Probably not. It may threaten you, but they rarely bite, especially a baby. Sorry, Estelle." Maddy lowers her voice. "I woke my roommate. It's more likely to just go limp, but be careful all the same, okay?"

"It did that when I picked it up."

"Now, pay attention, there's a gap between the incisors and molars, called the diastema. You put your finger in the gap and pry its mouth open. Once you get it clean, feed it. Wet cat food will work. Go to my house—"

"I'm at your house."

"Good. There's a small cage in the storeroom. Put it in that with a heating pad from the closet in the back bedroom and keep it for a couple of days until it's clearly eating on its own. Got it?"

"I think so."

"Call me in the morning."

"I will."

I shut myself in the bathroom with a roll of paper towels and a toothpick. I sit on the floor with my back against the tub and my knees drawn up, holding the baby in my left hand, letting my knees support my arm and its back legs. I start by cleaning the goop out of the plugged nostril with the blunted end of the toothpick. When the baby is no longer snuffling and air is moving freely in and out, I begin pulling the pine needles off its toes. All the time I'm working, it holds perfectly still, eventually relaxes and even closes *his* eyes. I've finally noticed it doesn't have a pouch.

I give us both a rest every five or ten minutes, cradle him and stroke his head and his soft, veined, transparent ears. His pointy face with its crossed eyes is so ugly, I begin to love him.

The cats sniff at the base of the door. Risty sticks her paw under it and feels around. I tap the top of her paw, which she turns pads up and claws ready.

I wrap a finger with a paper towel, stick my finger in the gap Maddy described, and pry open the possum's mouth. Strands of slime stretch from lip to lip and crisscross his whole mouth. I wrinkle my nose, take a deep breath, hook a bit of slime, and pull. Long strands stick to the toweling. I rip off another sheet and do it again.

I'm not sure how much time has passed, but the basket by the toilet is full of paper towels. The slime never seems to end. Every ten minutes or so, I give his jaws a rest to work on his feet—pulling as gently as I can on his little toes. Never, not once, even after I get his mouth clean enough to expose his sharp, spiky teeth, does he threaten me, or fight me.

When his feet are clean, and his mouth dried out, I put him in the bathtub, close the door, and go to the kitchen to get a flashlight. The clock on the oven reads 11:45.

The entrance to the storeroom where Maddy keeps spare cages is outside and around behind the house. I find a medium-size carrier. When I get back, the bathroom door is open. I charge in. All three cats are lined up, standing with their front paws on the side of the tub, staring at the baby possum, which is backed against the far side of the tub, showing all its needle teeth.

"Out."

Only Rufus obeys.

I put the cage on the toilet and clap my hands together. "Out."

Risty and Cory zip out, and I close the door.

I find the heating pad in the back-bedroom closet and get rags from on top of the washing machine. When I come out, the bathroom door is pushed open again, and the cats are sitting on the side of the tub. I reach over them, but before I can pick up the possum, he sags against the side of the tub, pretending to have died. I pick him up and put him in the carrier. Rufus jumps into the tub, and sniffs where the possum peed. Cory and Risty follow me to the kitchen.

I plug in the heating pad, add a layer of rags in case the low setting is too hot, then lift the possum and put it in the bottom of the cage. I get a small dish from under the stove to hold the food that the cats haven't eaten. I also cut up a carrot—the only vegetable left that hasn't rotted.

Since the cats can push open the bathroom door, I leave the carrier on the kitchen counter. The door is latched. Even if they jump up to look at him, they can't hurt him.

The baby possum stays in a ball in the back of the cage until he smells the food. He slowly uncurls, wobbles to the front, and begins to eat.

I clean up the bathroom, wipe out the tub, and burn the paper towels in the woodstove. By now, it's too late to go home, and since neither Cindee nor Stan called to check on me, I spend the night in Maddy's recliner with Rufus on my stomach. When I wake the next morning, the possum is curled into a ball, asleep. I watch his side rise and fall. That night, when I give him the leftover cat food, he hisses at me and bares his tiny, sharp teeth.

"So much for gratitude." I put the food inside the cage door, unplug the heating pad, and put in a water dish. The baby is wolfing down the cat food when I reach past him. He doesn't react, so I stroke the top of his head with a finger. He stops eating, closes his eyes, and lets himself be touched.

Tuesday night I feed the baby, then carry his cage outside. "No more slugs," I warn, and open the door. He lifts his head and sniffs his way to the edge of the cage, tumbles out, and dives under the front deck.

CHAPTER 18

I

On Wednesday morning, Cindee and I pull up at the rear entrance to Sherwood Oaks. I go in alone because Cindee doesn't want to get involved reminiscing with past coworkers. She waits in the car with her classic rock station turned up. When I glance back at her, Cindee's eyes are closed and she's waving her arms above her head in time with whatever song is playing. I can't hear the music, which makes her look more demented than some of the old people in their wheelchairs inside.

II

Are you excited to be coming home?" Cindee smiles at Maddy, who's sitting next to her as we creep down Oak Street.

"Very, and thank you for picking me up. I told Finch I could just have easily called Dial-A-Ride."

"Finch?"

"Maddy calls me Finch."

"How odd," says Cindee. "Anyway, I wouldn't think of

letting you take a bus home." She smiles again. "We're all so glad the good Lord saw fit to keep you with us for a while longer."

I swallow a giggle when Maddy turns to look at Cindee. "If he was being generous with my time here on earth, why'd he push me off the roof in the first place?"

This gets a startled laugh out of Cindee. "You don't think the Lord caused you to fall, do you?"

"No, I don't."

"I'm relieved." Cindee pats Maddy's arm.

"And I don't think some higher power stuck a fork in me and decided I wasn't done yet." Maddy pats Cindee's arm. "I hope you aren't risking your eternal soul giving me a lift home."

"It's not *my* soul we need to worry about." Cindee swings into Maddy's driveway, narrowly missing her mailbox, and rolls to a stop at the end of the walkway to the front door. I jump out, get Maddy's walker from the trunk, and open it beside the passenger door. Maddy lifts her right leg over the doorframe, then her left.

Cindee keeps the motor running and stares straight ahead.

With my help, Maddy stands up. "I'll be home in a little while," I tell Cindee, and shut the car door. Cindee, with the tires spitting gravel, steers a tight loop, drives to the top of the hill, and turns out onto the road.

"Sorry, Finch, I couldn't resist. Whenever someone starts talking about God and my eternal soul, memories of my mother creep back. She was narrow-minded, hateful, bigoted, and self-righteous. More religious than Christian. Get her started on how other people should live their lives, and she was the Lord's right-hand woman."

"It's okay, Maddy. I thought it was kind of funny. She prays about every little thing. If everyone is praying for silly stuff, like winning a football game, or that the store isn't out of grapefruit, how does God have time to deal with important stuff—like sick people?"

I help Maddy settle in her recliner and go to the kitchen to heat water for tea. "Look who's coming." Maddy points out the window.

The dog trots down the driveway.

"You've done a good job, Finch. He looks nice and healthy."

When the dog sees her, he stops and stares, then stretches his front paws like he's going to lie down, but his butt stays in the air and his tail wags.

"From him, that's quite a welcome." Maddy puts her hand against the glass.

The dog tucks his tail and pins his ears but stays put.

"He only stays close if the window's between us."

"Until we gain his trust, we won't be able to get that rope off his neck, and it's tighter now that he's gained weight."

I look at my feet, full of guilt. He might be tame by now if I hadn't scared him that day.

Maddy puts her head back and closes her eyes. A moment later all three cats jump in her lap. She yelps and flinches, but strokes each of them in turn.

III

Stan and Cindee are in the kitchen when I come in from Maddy's. They turn to look at me. Stan is holding Cindee's credit card bill. "Do you know anything about this charge?"

My stomach does a flip-flop. "What charge?"

"Ninety-five cents to Intelius." He hands me the statement.

The Walmart charge for $16.95 plus shipping is also there, but he hasn't mentioned it. He probably thinks it's something Cindee bought. It's not the only Walmart charge. I hand it back to him. "What's the big deal?"

"If you didn't make this charge, we need to report that someone has her credit card number and is using it."

"You'd better do that, then." I start for my room.

"Intelius is a people-finder search engine. Who were you looking for?"

I reach into my pocket, pull out a crumpled dollar bill, stomp back to the kitchen, and slap it down on the counter. "Here's her ninety-five cents with interest."

"Don't move." Stan's voice is low and even.

When I look at him, he shakes his head. "That's not the point, Morgan. You stole her credit card number."

"I didn't steal anything. I borrowed it."

"If you didn't ask permission, it isn't borrowing. Who were you looking for?"

"Who do you think?" I snap. "My real father." I cross the living room, go down the hall and into my room. I slam the door as hard as I can. I throw myself across my bed and wait for the door to fly open.

Nothing. Just the murmur of their voices in the kitchen.

I must have dozed off, because a quiet tapping on my door wakes me. "What?"

"May I come in?" It's Stan.

He doesn't sound mad anymore, but I want him to think I am. "Whatever."

He opens the door. I'm always surprised at how tall he is. His head just clears the doorjamb.

He comes to stand at the foot of my bed but doesn't say anything for several moments. His fingers rub a small square of folded paper. "Cindee says I should give this to you."

"What is it?"

Stan doesn't answer, just leans and hands it to me.

How I know what it is, I'm not sure, but my heart rockets in my chest as I unfold the paper.

Morgan Delgado, 2072 Bass Ct., Eureka, CA 707-555-4326.

I look up at Stan. "How long have you had this?"

"Since your mother died."

"Why didn't you give it to me?"

"You never asked."

I read it again. It's in Stan's handwriting. "How did you get it?"

"He called after your mom passed."

"He called?" I slam my fist against the mattress. "He called here?" I shout. "Why didn't you tell me? Why didn't you let me talk to him?"

"He didn't— I think you were in school."

"Why did he call if not to talk to me?"

Stan sighs and sits down on the side of my bed. "He said he left some tools here and wanted to know if I was using them."

"Tools?"

Stan nods. "I told him I'd look for them, but I never did."

"Did he ask about me?"

Stan stares at his hands, which are on his knees. "Sure he did. I told him you were fine."

"I'm not fine. I want to see him."

"Not a good idea, Morgan. Things have changed with him."

"He's my father. Nothing can change that."

"That's just biology. His . . . his circumstances—"

"What does that mean?" I roll off the other side of the bed and stand. "I don't care about his circumstances. He's my father, and you have no right to keep us apart. Why didn't you tell me he'd called? Did he want to come back? Were you afraid we'd throw you two out? Was that it?"

Stan looks punched, but I don't let that stop me. "Was that it?"

"He has no interest . . ."

"No interest in what?"

"Nothing." He stands and walks to the door.

"What if he finds out you don't have a job and got a DUI? What then? Huh? Does he know I'm living with a drunk?"

Stan's jaw muscles tighten, but his voice is soft. "Just because you're having a meltdown, don't say things you will live to regret, Morgan. Call him and find out for yourself how deeply he cares about . . . about any of this." He walks a few feet down the hall, turns, and comes back. "One other thing: if you slam another door in this house, I'll take the damn thing off its hinges."

CHAPTER 19

I

n the back of the bathroom medicine cabinet are Boo
Boo Kisses adhesives in shades of orange, red, pink,
and purple. They've been there since I got poison oak
when I was seven. I choose the bright red lips and stick my
father's address and phone number to the mirror over my
dresser.

That night I fall asleep imagining the excitement in his
voice when he answers the phone. "Oh my God, Morgan,
I've missed you so much. Not a day goes by I don't think of
you," he'll say. "How would you like to live in Eureka?"

Each day my mind creates new scenarios. By the end
of the week, he's breaking down in sobs of gratitude and
relief that I've forgiven him for leaving.

I don't go to the creek to tell my mother. I'm afraid there's
a voice waiting there to remind me he left when we needed
him most. And I don't tell Maddy. She'll try to prepare me
to be disappointed.

School's out for Thanksgiving, so I call Sherri's cell and
leave a message that I found him, and to please call me.
She doesn't. Maybe they've gone somewhere for the holiday,

or maybe she's sorry she said she and Deanne would take me to see him. Days go by.

ll

On the Saturday morning after Thanksgiving, when I come off the trail, I find Maddy waiting for me. If her hip didn't still hurt, I imagine her foot would be tapping impatiently. I look at my watch. It's 7:50. On school days I'm there by 6:30 to help her feed the animals, but she can't be upset that I slept later than I do on weekdays.

"What wrong?"

"We've got a rescue. Can you drive a car?"

I shrug. "Sort of. I drove Stan to the Mobil station for beer a couple weeks ago."

"That's enough practice. The house is just off Sequoia. Less than a mile."

I'm happy to see her excited and more like her old self, but my heart flutters a bit. "Okay, but I've only driven that once . . . and Stan helped steer."

"We'll be fine."

"What are we going to get?"

"Bats."

"Really?" *Cool.* "Are they hurt?"

"No, but they will be if we don't hurry. The people who own the house want them killed, but David, their gardener, called me."

I see a birdhouse and a pair of gloves in the backseat as I help Maddy into her Prius. "What's the birdhouse for?"

"We need something to carry them home in. When we

get back, you can hang it in the woodshed. They'll fly off when they're ready."

I've ridden in her Prius, but never paid attention to how she starts it or changes gears. Once I get the seat pushed back far enough for my legs, I wait for the key.

"Put your foot on the brake and push the Power button," she instructs.

All the lights on the dash glow but there's still no engine sound. "What am I doing wrong?"

"Nothing. It's running. Keep your foot on the brake, and move the lever to D."

I do, and without a sound the Prius starts to roll. It's not until I put my foot on the gas pedal that the engine finally shudders and the car begins to climb the driveway. I grin at Maddy.

At the top of the driveway, I stop to look for traffic.

"Clear this way," Maddy says.

I give it gas—a bit too much—and we zoom out of the driveway. I cut the wheel to the left in time to keep from running off the other side of the road.

"Lord love a duck," Maddy gasps, her hand at her chest.

"I told you I couldn't drive."

"We're not in the ditch, so don't worry about it. Applying just the right amount of gas takes experience. You'll get the hang of it. Go to Sequoia and turn right."

I've only ridden in regular cars: Sherri's Mustang, Cindee's Honda, and Stan's huge 4×4 truck with a faded bumper sticker on the back that reads "Save a Logger, Eat a Spotted Owl." The Prius is hard to get used to. It shudders and seems to die at every stop.

Sequoia narrows where it passes the north end of McDowell Creek. There's a car coming from the east, and I don't want to pass it when the whole road looks the width of a pencil. I wait until it goes by before I make the turn and center the Prius in the middle of the road.

Maddy's looking out the window and checking house numbers against a ragged piece of paper. "Must be in the next block."

Another car is coming. I pull over until it looks like I'm off the road on Maddy's side, stop, and wait for it to pass. The driver smiles.

"You've got lots of room on this side. Don't be nervous."

"I'm trying."

"Haven't you taken driver's ed yet?"

"Not until the tenth grade. I'm in sixth."

Maddy looks at me. "After all that's happened, I forget you're still so young. Oops. There it is. Back up."

"I don't know how to back up."

"Put it in reverse and look over your shoulder."

I put the car in reverse and creep backward along the road until I see a truck coming up behind us. I look in the side-view mirror on Maddy's side, where it says in pale letters, "Objects in mirror are closer than they appear." *Great.*

"You're fine," Maddy says. "Turn left."

I forget to put it in drive, so when I step on the gas and turn the wheel, the rear end swings into the path of the oncoming truck. The driver blasts his horn and swerves around me on the right, bounces off the pavement, and mows down a huckleberry bush before getting back onto the pavement. He gives me the finger and keeps going.

I put my head against the steering wheel.

"That was my fault." Maddy pats my shoulder. "I didn't see the truck coming and I didn't remind you to change gears, or to put your turn signal on."

At the house, Maddy shakes hands with the man who called about the bats. "¿Cómo está, David? Esta es mi amiga, Finch."

David shakes my hand.

"Sorry, I don't speak Spanish," I say, "but it's nice to meet you."

"The bats are in the shed," David says, and crooks a finger for us to follow.

"The best thing would be to put them back where you found them," Maddy tells him.

"Owner say no. Wants me to kill them."

"Stupid people."

"I rescued them for you."

Maddy pats his shoulder. "You're a good man."

David opens the door to a toolshed. It's dark inside. He pulls the string to a single bulb in the ceiling and points to a pair of short boards, one on top of the other, lying on a coiled garden hose.

I glance at Maddy, worried that he may have accidentally squished them. There isn't a millimeter of space between the boards.

"Let me have the gloves, Finch."

"I can pick them up, Maddy."

"No. If one of us is bitten, I want it to be me." Maddy pulls on the heavy gloves. For the first time I notice how skinny and white her left arm is from the weeks in a cast. "Take the bottom out of the birdhouse and hold it so I can put them inside."

I push up on the bottom, turn the square of wood sideways, and remove it. "Ready," I say.

David lifts the top board. Three tiny bats are snuggled together in a clump on the bottom board.

"Little brown bats. My favorite," Maddy says.

Every living thing is her favorite.

She picks up the first one and gently presses it to the inside wall of the birdhouse, then the next two. "Put the bottom in, Finch." She takes off the gloves, and jams one into the entrance hole. "There we go. We'll take them home and enjoy a mosquito-free summer."

I do better driving home until the first bat lands on the dashboard. I slam on the brakes, and we both turn and look in the backseat. There's a gap between the body of the birdhouse and its slanted roof. The last bat's head appears in the gap, and it joins the others as they fly around the inside of the car. "What should I do?" I say.

Maddy starts to laugh. "You're not scared, are you?"

"No."

"Then drive on, Macduff."

"Won't they hit the window? Or get in our hair?"

"No. They're using echolocation, so these windows are like a brick wall to them. And they have no interest in our hair."

The bat that landed on the dash flies between us and lands on the back headrest.

I slowly start again, and the bats continue to flutter around the inside of the car. There's someone at the stop sign on the corner of McDowell Creek and Sequoia waiting to turn left. I put on my signal, and slow to make the turn. Out of the corner of my eye, I see the woman look at us and smile, then blink. Her mouth drops open and her eyes bug as we go by with three bats circling.

Maddy's laughing so hard she begins to cough. I start to laugh until I'm afraid I'm going to wet my pants.

When I park at the bottom of Maddy's drive, she's still trying to catch her breath. "Put the back windows down."

I do, and a second later, all three bats fly out and straight into the woods.

Maddy holds her right hand up and we high-five. "This should be our little secret, don't you agree?"

"I'll never tell."

Maddy pats my cheek. "It's wonderful to see you laugh."

"You, too."

"I sure hope my stitches held."

CHAPTER 20

Sherri hasn't been in school for a week and hasn't returned my three calls. I've been taking the bus since the Thanksgiving break ended. Sometimes I see the red Mustang in the driveway and other days I don't. My feelings are hurt, but at least I know they haven't moved away.

Winter recess starts in two weeks. That's when I want to go see my father, but I don't know if Sherri's promise about Deanne driving me was just smoke. On Saturday, I tell Cindee I'm going to Maddy's, but I don't want Maddy to know I'm sneaking off to Sherri's so I don't get the bike from her shed. I walk until I'm out of sight of either house to put my thumb out.

The first car by is a man. When he smiles and slows, I put my arm behind my back and shake my head. The next car I hear before I see it. It's coming very fast. I put my hand behind my back. The third car is a woman. She eyes me suspiciously but stops.

"How far you going?"

"To a friend's on Sequoia."

"Aren't you the Delgado girl?"

"Yes, ma'am."

"It's dangerous to hitchhike."

"I'm careful. I waited for a lady."

"That's good, but still—"

When she lets me off across the street from Sherri's, I see a blond woman I assume is Sherri's mom, and a man, who must be Jake, getting into the Mustang. They lean in and kiss each other before he starts the engine.

I wait until they drive away and I'm about to cross the road when I spot Sherri at the living room window. She seems to be looking right at me, so I wave. She doesn't wave back, and after a few seconds, lets the curtain drop.

I'm confused. I don't know why she doesn't want to see me but can't bring myself to go knock on the door. I walk back up the hill until I'm out of sight of her house before sticking out my thumb for a ride home.

The next morning, I decide to find out what's going on. After I feed Otus and Rav for Maddy, I risk being interrogated and ask her if it's okay to take the bike to a friend's house.

She's in her recliner with her eyes closed. She really did hurt herself laughing about the bats, and she's in pain again.

"Sure," she says. Before her accident she would have quizzed me on who this friend is and what we were planning to do.

"Maddy, you're okay, right?"

She opens her eyes. "Of course I am, sweetie. Just a bit achy."

I slow near Sherri's house. The Mustang is in the driveway. I get off the bike and pretend to check one of the tires.

The screen door slams. "Finch."

I feel stupid for letting Sherri see me stop right opposite her house again. I pretend not to hear her, get back on the bike, and start to ride away.

"Finch. Wait."

I hear her running toward me.

"Please wait."

I stop, turn the bike to face her, and cross my arms over my chest like I'm mad.

Sherri's cool is gone. She stands at the end of the driveway, her arms at her side, palms open. Her blue-streaked hair is matted and shows about two inches of brown roots. She's wearing a ragged sweatshirt and sweatpants, and her feet are bare. "I'm sorry," she says, and steps onto the road.

"Watch out!"

A car swerves around Sherri and nearly hits me.

Sherri looks both ways this time and runs across the road. "Are you okay?"

"Are you?"

Sherri shrugs. "It's been a bad couple of weeks."

"Like what?"

"You don't want to know."

There's a yellowing bruise under her left eye. I catch her chin to make her look at me. "What's that?"

Her shoulders sag. "It's not what you think." She glances at the house. "They had a big fight on Thanksgiving and I got in the middle. Mom threw a beer bottle at Jake, missed, and hit me. She had us packing to move, but now they've made up."

We stand there. I'm looking up the road; she's looking the other direction. "Whatcha been—?" we say in unison.

"Nothing," we both answer.

I swallow my pride. "Did you see me yesterday? I waved."

"When?"

"Your mom and Jake were kissing in the car."

Sherri shakes her head. "Where were you?"

"Right here. I came by to see if you were okay. You haven't been to school."

"Mom made me stay home. She was afraid the school would call CPS if they saw my eye."

"Why didn't you answer my calls?"

Sherri looks at her feet to keep from looking at me. "I didn't want you to see me, either."

"You're my best friend. I've missed—"

Tears well and she hugs me. "I've missed you, too."

"I found my real father," I say when she lets go of me.

"No way. Was he happy to see you?"

"I haven't talked to him yet."

"Why not?"

I shake my head. "I'm scared to call him, but he only lives in Eureka."

"Are you going up to see him?"

"How would I do that?"

"I told you Deanne would take you."

"I forgot," I lie, but am so happy she remembers. I glance at the Mustang. What would my father think if I showed up on his doorstep in a red convertible? "Would your mother let you guys take the car that far?"

"Not if she's here, which she won't be. The happy couple is going to Las Vegas for a week. I think they're getting married."

"That's cool."

Sherri snorts a laugh. "She's been married four times, so I don't know how cool it is." She takes my hand. "Mom's leaving us a credit card to buy gas and food. Maybe we could use it to stay overnight in a motel. One with a heated pool."

The mention of a motel pool makes me think of Laytonville. My stomach flutters. "I don't know."

"Why not? We'll have a blast."

"What if they have another fight?"

"Even if they do, we could skip school, drive to Eureka, and be back the same day. Mom would never know we'd been gone."

"What will your mom do when the credit card bill comes in?"

Sherri shrugs. "Too late for her to do anything by then."

"I guess I could tell Cindee and Stan I was sleeping over at your house."

"Perfect. The minute they leave, I'll call you."

||

Deanne took the car in to be serviced, so Sherri and I have to take the bus home from school on Friday. Amanda and Lacey are in the first row so we go to the back. We've just come off the circle onto Sequoia when Amanda shouts, "Hey, Morgan, isn't that your father?"

Like a wave at a football game, starting at the front of the school bus, kids get up to look out the window, and laugh. Those sitting on the other side of the bus cross the aisle to see Stan riding our lawn mower up the bike lane on Sequoia. Two six-packs of beer are on the floor between his feet and a plastic Safeway bag swings on the handlebar. Out the filthy rear window of the bus I watch him wave away the diesel fumes. I turn in my seat, wishing I were invisible. Safeway is five miles from home. By now the whole town must have seen him.

"New car?" Amanda snickers.

Everyone laughs.

"He's not my father!" I shout. I always let Amanda get to me, but this cuts too deep. I stand even though I'm not sure what I'm going to do. Sherri grabs my wrist and pulls me back down in the seat.

"What *is* your freaking problem?" she yells at Amanda.

"None of your beeswax."

Sherri gets up and marches up the aisle toward Amanda. I jump up and follow.

"Sit down!" the driver shouts. She's watching us in the rearview mirror.

Sherri ignores her. The bus slows and stops.

"I said sit down." The driver turns and points at us.

"I'm just gonna sit here with my friend." Sherri jerks Lacey out of the seat next to Amanda and sits down. I sit behind them. The driver watches for a minute, then the bus begins to roll again.

Amanda looks nervous. She faces Sherri with her back pressed to the window.

"I'm asking you again. What *is* your problem?"

Amanda shrugs. "I don't like her."

"Why?"

She shrugs again. "She's too tall."

Sherri looks over the seat back at me. "There you have it." She turns her palms up. "You're too tall."

I nod because I can't think quick enough to say anything clever.

Sherri smiles. "On the flip side, Amanda-panda, I don't like you, because you're so short. It's sad because you will never get any bigger than you are right now."

"What does that mean?"

"You're a nasty person and nasty stunts your growth. It's a fact." Sherri pats Amanda's shoulder sympathetically, and reaches her other hand, palm up, back to me.

I low-five it.

III

Cindee's lying in bed, propped up on four pillows. The TV's on and she's watching a game show.

"We passed Stan riding the lawn mower. Why would you let him do that?"

"I feel awful. Thanks for asking."

"Everyone saw him."

"The doctor called in a prescription for me. He went to pick it up."

"Couldn't he have driven this once?"

"Every cop in Fort Bragg knows Stan. If he got caught, they'd take his license for good."

"Doesn't Safeway deliver?"

"None of the pharmacies do."

"I was so embarrassed, I wanted to die."

"You'll get over it." Cindee blows her nose like a semi's air horn and throws the tissue into the paper bag beside her bed. "Empty that, will you?"

"I don't want to touch it. It's full of germs."

"I didn't ask you to touch them. Put the whole thing in the woodstove, get another paper bag from the pantry, and fix me a cup of tea while you're at it. Chamomile, pretty please."

"Hey, babe. How ya feeling?" Stan's in the doorway.

"Better now that you're home."

"Everyone on the school bus saw you riding up Sequoia," I say.

"Why would I care what a load of pimply faced brats saw?"

"They made fun of me."

"Toughen up, Morgan." Stan takes a bottle of pills from the Safeway bag. "Go get Cindee some more water."

I grab the glass off the bedside table and go into the bathroom to refill it.

"Take two now, then one a day for the next three days. They're heavy-duty antibiotics." He looks in the bag, then down at her and smiles. "I brought you a present."

"What?" She claps her hands together like a two-year-old.

Stan pulls a tabloid from the bag. "The new *National Enquirer.*"

"You're too good to me. Thank you, honey."

He leans and kisses her clown-red nose. "What else can I get you?"

My hand starts to shake, slopping water onto the carpet. What I see is not Cindee, but my mother lying there, and Stan leaning over to kiss her.

"Morgan's going to make me some tea."

Stan looks at me and smiles once more. "That's nice."

I put the glass of water on the bedside table and leave. I run out the door and across the yard. The dog is in Maddy's yard when I come off the trail. By the time I reach my trees, he's on the deck watching me. He lies down and puts his head on his paws. It makes me feel guarded.

CHAPTER 21

I

We're going to Eureka this weekend. I can't sleep for fear something will go wrong. My biggest worry was whether Stan would want to talk to Sherri's mother before letting me go there to spend the night. It did occur to him, but Cindee intervened.

"Don't be a curmudgeon. He never asks to do anything with friends."

Later, Cindee catches me in the kitchen. "You're not off to some party, are you?" Her cold is hanging on, and her nose is still stopped up.

"No. We're just going to listen to music and play video games."

"Promise?"

"I promise. We're not going to a party."

"I'm glad you've found a little friend."

A little friend? Like I'm five.

I tell Maddy the same story, and feel guilty because she, too, believes me. "Don't rush home to feed the animals. I can manage if I go slow."

"Thanks, Maddy. I probably will stay and go to a movie tomorrow afternoon."

Thankfully, she doesn't ask what's playing, because I don't know.

I put my old bathing suit, my pajamas, a hairbrush, toothpaste, and a toothbrush in a paper sack in the main section of my backpack. I don't own a suitcase and haven't slept a night away from this house except when Mom was in the hospital to have first one breast removed, then the other. Dad slept in a chair in her room and I stayed with Maddy.

The last time I slept at Maddy's was after Mom died and the funeral home took her away. When Stan came to get me the next morning, he was still drunk. Maddy wouldn't let me go home with him and kept me with her for another night.

I stand in the doorway to my closet trying to think what else I'll need. The shoebox with my keepsakes is on the top shelf. I take it down and carry it to my bed, thinking I'll take a couple of things to show Dad, but I can't decide what to leave. I want him to know I've kept everything he left behind.

Cindee's napping; Stan's in the woods. I go to the kitchen for a Ziploc to put everything in, but find a dark blue velvet Crown Royal bag in one of the drawers. It has a gold drawstring. Inside are Scrabble tiles.

I take them to the kitchen counter and pour them out onto a newspaper so I don't wake Cindee. Just the letters; there's no board. It broke in half years ago, but Mom kept the letters and used them to help teach me to spell. We would sit on stools opposite each other, with the letters spread out between us. I chose a word—like "lamp" or "chair," and together we found the letters to spell it.

I begin to select letters and arrange them on the counter. I L-O-V-E Y-O-U M-O-M. I don't care if Cindee and Stan see it. I'm going to be with my real father. I scrape the rest of the letters into a Ziploc, leave my message on the counter, and take the Crown Royal bag.

II

After I feed Otus and Rav, I go up to the road—out of sight of either house—to hitch a ride. The dog is sitting on the other side of the road watching me. He's started hanging around all day now that Maddy is home. He arrives in the morning, and watches her through the windows, circling the house to keep her in view. After his evening meal, he goes back to where his people left him.

III

I get a ride—this time in an ancient orange Ford pickup with an old man and his dog. The dog—a black Lab mix—sits between us in the front seat and keeps sniffing my ear. His nose is cold, and it makes me want to giggle.

The old man lets me out at the end of Sherri's driveway, tips his John Deere cap, and rumbles on down the road. Deanne and Sherri are leaning on the hood of the Mustang studying a map, the four corners of which are held down by an overnight bag, two rocks, and a small cooler.

"See what you think," Sherri says.

I look at the map. "About what?"

"Should we drive up the coast, which will take longer

but be beautiful, or go over Highway 20 and take 101 North?"

"Up the coast." I've never been farther than MacKerricher State Park, about seven miles north. Mom took me there to see a flock of migrating swans that arrived one fall and stayed two days before moving on.

"Good." We high-five.

Sherri and I sit in the back like Deanne's our chauffeur. The top is down. Between the wind and the radio turned up and booming, we can't hear to talk. After Westport the twisty road through the trees straightens and we can see all the way to the mountains of the Lost Coast.

Now that the road is straighter, Deanne's driving faster.

"You know we're freezing back here, right?" Sherri shouts.

Deanne turns the radio down. "What?"

"We're freezing."

At the next vista point, she pulls over. They get the top up, but it takes all three of us hanging on it to get it latched down.

"How long since you've seen your father?" Deanne asks.

"I was eight."

"Wow. He won't know who you are."

"I know."

For years I imagined seeing my father walking toward me on a street in Fort Bragg, or shopping in the same aisle at Harvest Market. I watch him approach, waiting for the moment he recognizes me. When he does, his face lights up and he sweeps me into his arms and hugs me so hard I can hardly breathe.

Fog lies thinly against the steep cliffs. Here and there are patches of deep blue ocean dotted with towering offshore rocks. I know from Maddy that they were once part of the coastline, now eroded down to sea stacks covered with bird poop.

"Do you ever talk to your father?" I ask them.

"Hell no." Sherri looks at her sister. "And I never want to."

I lean forward. "Why do you say that?"

"He left our mother the minute he found out she was pregnant with Sherri. Another damn mouth to feed, he said. Why would either of us want to see him?"

"I don't know. Because he's blood?"

"Cold blood," Sherri says.

"Why do you want to see yours?" Deanne asks.

"My memories of him are pretty good."

"He left her mom when she got sick," Sherri tells her sister.

"Yeah, but just to find a better job. He said he'd be back. Mom should have waited and not married Stan."

"Has he tried to get in touch with you?" Deanne says.

"He called twice that I know of, but he could have called lots of times and they didn't tell me."

Strands of fog drift up and across the road. They swirl around us as we speed through, torn apart and sent flying by our momentum. I put my head against the seat back and let the reunion with Dad play out in my mind again.

CHAPTER 22

According to MapQuest, Eureka is 133 miles north of Fort Bragg. We left the coast an hour ago and have been driving through giant redwoods for an hour and a half. I'm beginning to think we missed a turn-off or something. "Did you check to see how long it takes to get there?" I ask Deanne.

"I don't really care how long it takes. Do you?"

I definitely do. My mouth is dry and my stomach is in knots, but I say, "I guess not."

"We need gas." Deanne glances at me in the rearview mirror. "We'll stop in Garberville and ask, okay?"

While Sherri fills the tank, I go into the mini-mart to buy chips and sodas and ask how much farther to Eureka.

"About an hour." The woman behind the counter hands me my change. She's watching a customer in the big convex mirror at the back of the store.

I look at the clock behind her head. It's already three thirty.

"What'd she say?" Sherri says when I get back in the car.

"An hour."

"You excited?"

"Kind of. Maybe I should have called first. He might have moved, or he could be at work."

"I've gotta pee," Sherri says.

"Me, too." I climb out again.

We get the key from the lady behind the counter. Sherri goes first and I wait outside. When it's my turn, I'm washing my hands and glance at myself in the cracked bathroom mirror.

My hair is in a windblown ponytail. I can't let my father see me as a girl. I open the door. Deanne has pulled the car over in front of the bathrooms. Sherri's in the backseat.

"Did either of you bring a pair of scissors?"

They look at each other and shake their heads.

"I can't show up with my hair like this. I have to cut it off."

"Why?" they say in unison, then Sherri gets it. "Never mind," she says to Deanne. "We'll find a drugstore and buy a pair."

"It doesn't look that bad," Deanne says. "Just brush it."

Sherri smiles at me. "The last time Finch saw her dad, she had really short hair. She wants him to recognize her."

I hug her and climb into the backseat. She's even kept my secret from her sister.

Sherri uses her sister's cell phone to Google drugstores in Garberville and gets directions to Pharmacy Express inside Ray's Food Place. Deanne waits in the car with the radio playing. Sherri and I go in, buy scissors, and go to the restroom. I pull off the scrunchie and put it in the bag with the receipt for the scissors.

"You sure?"

I nod and blink back tears. "He's got to think I'm his son, not a Nancy boy like he used to call me."

"He thought you were gay?"

"Uh-huh. Mom did, too."

"Are you?" Sherri gathers my hair in her fist.

I'd never really thought about it. "I don't know."

"It's simple. Would you rather date a boy or a girl?"

"A boy."

"Then you're straight because you're a girl." She holds up the scissors. "Ready?"

When I nod a single tear dislodges and splashes in the rust-stained sink.

She cuts my ponytail off at the nape of my neck and hands it to me. Then she trims the long sides and around my ears. I watch in the mirror as my hair drifts to the floor. "Do you want bangs?"

"I hate bangs." I take the scissors from her, part and comb some hair forward, hesitate, then cut a straight line across my forehead.

Sherri uses damp paper towels to clean up the hair on the floor, takes my ponytail from where I draped it over the rim of the sink, and dumps it in the trash can.

I stare at my reflection in the mirror, and then at Sherri standing behind me. Her expression says it all. She pats my shoulder. "It'll grow out."

"But everyone at school—"

"No, they won't. You look like a girl with short hair. When we get home, we'll style it, put some curl in it." She cocks her head. "But for now, you need to look more like a boy." She uses the bathroom soap to slick down the sides and to make my bangs stand up like the boys at school wear theirs. "There." She turns me back to face the mirror. "If you were really a boy, I'd want to date you."

I try to smile, but the face looking back at me makes me want to throw up.

When I climb into the backseat, Deanne gasps. "Oh my God. Why did you do that? You look like—" Her brow creases. "—a boy!" She looks at Sherri. "A boy?"

"I'm sorry. We should have told you."

"Don't be," Deanne says. "It's just a shock, that's all."

"I want to look the way my father remembers me."

"But are you a boy?" Deanne asks.

"She's trans," Sherri says.

"Does her father know?"

Sherri and I shake our heads.

Deanne starts the engine. "This should be good."

II

It's five thirty and nearly dark when we pull into Eureka. We stop at the first gas station and ask directions to the address Stan gave me. It's hard to find his place amid blocks and blocks of the shabby, closely spaced houses. We pass it twice before I spot our old Ford Explorer backed in between his house and the neighbor's.

Deanne parks across the street and cuts the engine. "Now what?"

His TV plays loudly, and I can see someone moving behind the sheet that covers the front window. My stomach feels filled with worms. "I don't know."

We stare at the house. "Maybe I could use your cell to

tell him I'm in town. Ask if it's okay to stop by and say hi."

"That's a good idea," Sherri says.

"I don't think so," Deanne says. "We've driven all this way. Don't give him a chance to say no. Make him say it to your face."

"My sister is such a pessimist." Sherri squeezes my hand. "I bet he's been hoping you'd show up and will want you to come live with him."

I'd love it if she was right, but the idiocy of this trip is making my heart pound. "He's known all along where I am."

"Yeah, but he's probably afraid that you hate him and hasn't had the nerve to ask you to forgive him."

"That's wishful thinking," Deanne says. "You hope that will happen to us one day. You should get over it. Our father's a piece of crap and so is hers—his—which is it?"

"Hers," Sherri says. "And you don't know what kind of man her dad is."

Maddy's sad-eyed face flashes in my mind. I blink it away and reach into my backpack for the Crown Royal bag. From it, I take the car key.

"What's that?" Sherri asks.

"The key to that car. I found it in a mud puddle in our driveway."

"What else is in that bag?"

"Stuff belonging to Dad that I've been saving." I hand Sherri his driver's license. She tilts it to catch the light from the lamppost.

A door slams, and my heart leaps like a bullfrog. A short, thin man in jeans and a white T-shirt steps out onto the porch. A match flares. He bends over cupped hands to light a cigarette. It's my father.

I don't remember opening the car door or climbing out. I stand in front of the car with my hand on the warm hood. I can't tell if he's looking at me or at the red Mustang.

"Morgan?" It's a woman's voice.

"What?" He sees me now and is looking at me with his head cocked like the dog does.

"Where are you?" the woman says.

"On the porch. What'd ya want?"

The door behind him opens and the light turns him into a silhouette. I can't see his face anymore.

"Who's that?"

"How should I know?"

I cross the road to stand at the curb in front of his house, their house. Is that his wife, or a girlfriend?

"What does he want?" the woman calls.

"Shut up," my father says. He comes down the steps, head still to one side. "Do I know you?"

I open my mouth but no sound comes out. I nod.

"See what he wants," the woman says.

My father turns. "Woman, I told you to shut up."

From inside the house, a baby starts to cry.

My knees get rubbery. I reach out to steady myself. My hand hits the red flag on the mailbox. I see "The Delgados, Morgan and Adrienne" stenciled on the side.

I back toward the car where Deanne and Sherri are waiting.

"Hey, wait a minute," my father says.

I stop.

His wife steps out onto the porch and is bouncing a baby, who is still screaming.

"Well, I'll be a monkey's uncle. Morgan? Is that you?"

"Hi, Dad." My voice quakes.

"Who is it?" Adrienne says.

"My son." He doesn't say it loud enough for her to hear, but his voice is warm and welcoming.

I blink back tears as he walks toward me, flicks away his burning cigarette, and puts his hands on my shoulders. He studies my face for a moment.

"Who is it?" she asks again.

"My son!" he shouts over his shoulder.

"Your what? You never told me about no other kid."

"Go in the *damn* house."

A child about three appears behind the screen. "Mommy, I'm hungry."

"What are you doing here?" Dad asks.

"I came to see you."

"Well, ain't that nice." He glances over his shoulder at his wife still standing on the porch. "I'd love to invite you in . . . you and your friends there, but the place is a mess. This one ain't the housekeeper your ma was." He cups his mouth like it's our little secret. "How old are you now?"

"Almost twelve."

"You didn't run away from home, did you?"

"No. My friends drove me up to see you."

"Nice. Real nice." He shakes his head. "Wow, it's hard to believe you're all grown up. And tall like your mom, but a handsome devil like your old man." He chuckles. I remember he used to do that instead of giving in to a full laugh.

There's a long pause when neither of us says anything. "How's your mom doing?"

The pavement rolls beneath my feet. "What do you mean?"

"Well, the cancer, you know?"

Why is he pretending he doesn't know? Stan said he called about his tools. Was Stan lying or was Mom's death so unimportant to him he's forgotten?

"She died, Dad."

"Well, hell's bells. I'm sorry to hear that." He has a pack of cigarettes rolled up in the sleeve of his undershirt. He takes one from the pack and lights it with a match from the book in his pants pocket. "How long ago?"

"Two years and two months."

"That's a real shame, that is."

He sucks smoke into his lungs and lets it drift out through his nose, coughs, turns his head and spits on the driveway.

The little girl at the screen door says again, "Mommy, I'm hungry."

"Shut up." Adrienne kicks the door with the heel of her shoe.

The little girl turns and runs down the hall.

"Is the baby a boy or a girl?" I say.

"A boy." My father glances over his shoulder at his wife and son.

Adrienne seems to take that as an invitation and comes down the steps. "Here, honey, can you take Junior? I need to start dinner." She stares at me, but Dad doesn't introduce us. She turns and goes back up the steps.

"Junior?"

Dad takes another drag off his cigarette and turns his head so as not to blow smoke in the baby's face. "Yeah, named him Morgan, too." He lowers his voice. "Wife there didn't know about you." He chuckles again. "Be hell to pay when supper's ready."

He holds the baby up, and sways with him like he's dancing, and suddenly I'm back at the pool in Laytonville. There's staticky music coming from a speaker on a post in the parking lot. I've been in the pool so long my lips are turning blue and my teeth chatter. Mom calls for me to get out, but it's Dad who comes to the side, holds a towel open for me, and wraps me in it when I come out of the water.

He dries me off, then picks me up, takes my right hand in his left, and begins to dance with me. I giggle as he whirls and dips so my head nearly touches the concrete. When he straightens, I hold on to his neck and put my head on his shoulder like I've seen Momma do when they dance in the kitchen to music on the radio. He holds my head in place with his big hand splayed across my wet hair and we dance around the pool, through the gate, and across the parking lot to our room.

"So, kiddo, was there something else, or did you just stop by to say hi?"

I jump. "What?"

He jiggles the baby and kisses the side of his head. "Was there something else?"

I don't know what to say. "I guess I thought you might like to come for a visit. Your family, too."

"Well, that would be real nice, that would. And I think I left some tools there I wouldn't mind having back. What's the guy's name your mom married?"

"Stan."

"That's right. Stan the Man." He makes a fist with his free arm and flexes his biceps.

"Stan remarried last year. My stepmom's nice, but, you know—" I shrug. "—they aren't blood."

He shakes his head. "Never the same."

I cross my fingers behind my back and kick the curb with the toe of my boot. "Maybe I could come up for a while this summer. Get to know my brother and sister."

"That there's something to consider, and I'd love it, really I would, but as you can see we got kind of a full house. The wife and me got two little ones and that don't leave much room to add to the mix, if you know what I mean. But I'll talk to her. Hope you understand."

"Sure. I understand."

"Well, I'm glad. I don't want you to think I wouldn't love to have you." He spits again—this time into the street. "What's in the bag?"

I had forgotten about the Crown Royal bag. "Just some things I've been saving." I open it, take out his penknife and put it in his hand, then his report card, his driver's license, their prom picture, and the car key.

He smiles at his picture and his grades. "Never was much of a student." He hands me the driver's license and report card, but stares for a moment at the prom picture, then hands it back, too.

"You're a beanpole like your mother was. That prom date with her was nearly our last." He flips the car key in the air like a coin and catches it. "I think this is the spare to the Explorer. Mind if I keep it, and the penknife? My last one got taken by some dude in airport security."

"I guess not."

My hand shakes as I put everything else back in the bag. "Dad?"

"Yeah?"

"Can I ask why you left us? Mom and me?"

"Well, you know," he says finally, "I'm not proud of it, but I was having problems dealing with her illness. The cancer and all. First one tit gone, then the other. I just couldn't live with that."

I feel as if a cold wind has come up. I can't believe this is who I thought would be the father I remember.

"She couldn't live with it, either." I back away, turn, and cross the road.

"Sorry, son," he says. "But hey, I sure am glad to see you didn't turn into a sissy Nancy boy."

I stop. My hand on the car door handle. I take a deep breath and square my shoulders.

"Don't be sorry, Dad." I turn. "The happiest year of Mom's life was after you left."

Sherri's out and holding the passenger seat forward for me to climb in.

"And Dad, don't worry about naming your son Morgan Jr. He's your only son. I'm your other daughter." I climb in and pull the seat back before Sherri can get in beside me. I want to be as alone as I can get.

Sherri shouts, "Jerkwad!" and gets in.

"Where to?" Deanne pulls away from the curb.

"Home," I say. "I don't want to spend another minute in the same town with him."

As we drive away, I take out the picture of Mom and Dad on prom night, tear my father's half off, hold it out the window, and watch it flap in the wind for a second before I let it go, then I open the Crown Royal bag, put my arm out, and shake it until the bag is empty.

CHAPTER 23

1

W e're only a couple blocks from Dad's house when I start to feel like I'm suffocating and the roof of the car is a coffin lid.

"Can we put the top down again?" My voice shakes.

Deanne looks at Sherri and pulls over. They unlatch the top. I push it the rest of the way down and pack it into the space behind my head, then sit with my hands pinned between my knees to keep them from shaking. Deanne puts the windows up and turns on the heater.

It's cold and the wind whips what's left of my hair, but I've gone numb, and am not paying attention when Deanne turns right off Myrtle Avenue onto Highway 101. We're halfway to Arcata before she realizes her mistake. It's a little after seven when we get back to Eureka.

The closer we get to the turn we took to my father's house, the harder it is to catch my breath. Pain spreads through my chest and I feel light-headed. Myrtle Avenue is the next light. I struggle out of my seat belt, get on my knees in the backseat, and let the cold wind punch me in the face. Tears stream into my ears.

At the light, Sherri crawls into the backseat and wraps her arms around me. "It'll be okay, Finch. I promise."

II

An hour later, we drive through Garberville looking for someplace to eat. We pass a couple of small, ratty-looking motels, but Sherri and Deanne decide their mother will probably not notice where she gassed up but will definitely notice a charge for a motel.

I spent the last of my cash on gas and snacks on the way north. Since none of us has any money left, we buy fried chicken at a service station and put it on the credit card with the gas. We eat what tastes like salty rubber in the glare of the fluorescent light pouring through the service station's front window.

I spit out a chunk of gristle. It lands on the pavement and reminds me of the glob of phlegm my father spat on his driveway. I look at Sherri. "Do you miss having a father?"

"Hell no," Deanne says.

Sherri's tone is kinder. "We've never had one, so we don't know what's to miss."

"Haven't any of your mother's boyfriends tried to be a father to you?"

Deanne laughs contemptuously. "Hardly."

|||

We've been back on the road for about thirty minutes when we pass a car with a headlight out.

"Padiddle!" Sherri smacks my arm.

"Ouch. What'd you do that for?"

"That car had a burned-out headlight."

"So?"

"First one to see it says 'padiddle' and gets to hit the other person."

"I don't want to play."

"Sure you do."

"No, I don't."

"Okay, but if only one of us is playing, you're going to take quite a beating." Sherri grins at me.

I turn my back to her, and then suddenly, in spite of myself, I laugh.

It's after midnight when they drop me off by our mailbox. "What are you going to say if they ask where you've been?"

I shrug. "If they notice I've been gone, they'll probably be disappointed that I came back."

When I come in, Stan's on a stool at the kitchen counter. Cindee's at the sink. They both turn and look at me.

"Hi." I cross the living room, headed for my bedroom.

"I thought you were—" Cindee says. "What are you doing home?"

"Where have you been?" Stan glances at the clock on the stove. "It's after midnight."

Before I close the door, I decide, why not? "Eureka."

"What did he say?"

"I think he said Eureka," Cindee says.

"Come back here!" Stan hollers.

"I'm going to bed."

"Bed can wait. You get in here and explain what you meant."

I stand for a moment in the bathroom doorway, take a deep breath, turn and walk to the kitchen. "Deanne and Sherri drove me to Eureka."

"Oh my God, your hair!" I watch Cindee figure out what happened. She puts her hand on Stan's arm. "Let him be."

"What do you mean, you drove to Eureka?" he yells, then blinks as if I'd swung my fist at him. "Did you go to your father's?"

I close my eyes. The next thing I know, Stan is hugging me, his chin on top of my head. I don't move, afraid he'll let go.

"I'm sorry," he whispers. "I should have warned you."

"You tried. I didn't believe you."

"I should have tried harder. Go on to bed. We'll talk in the morning."

IV

I come into the kitchen the next morning and Cindee turns from the sink, then walks over and puts her arms around me. "I'm sorry, too, Morgan."

I step away. Her arms feel like a closed trap. Life, here with them, is all I have.

She looks at me and I see the hurt. She drops her arms and walks back to the sink. "You want some breakfast?"

"No, and I don't ever want to be called Morgan again.

From now on, my name is Finch." I leave the house. From now on, my father is deader to me than my mother will ever be. About halfway across the yard, I start to run, and keep running until I reach my redwood bridge.

CHAPTER 24

F inch?" Maddy is standing on her back deck looking down at me. She cups her mouth with her hands.

I wipe my eyes with the heels of my hands and stand up. "Hi, Maddy." I wave and cross the bridge to her side of the creek.

"Cindee called."

"What'd she want?" I plod up the trail toward her.

"She said you were upset."

"She didn't tell you?" I hate how disappointed in me Maddy is going to be.

"Tell me what?"

"I went to see my father."

"Oh, Finch." Maddy shakes her head. "Come up here. Let's talk."

Maddy waits at the top of the hill for me. "Oh, honey," she says when she sees my hair. She opens her arms. I walk into them and start to cry.

"I'm so sorry, sweetheart. He's not a good man, but maybe it's just as well you found that out, rather than pining for the kind of father you're never going to have."

"I hate him."

"He isn't worth what it will cost you to hate him. Hate takes energy, and that man's not valuable enough to hate." Maddy pulls wads of tissues from her sweater pocket, selects a clean one, and hands it to me. "It takes so much effort to find your place in the world when you grow up angry. Let it go, sweetie."

Sunlight flickers through the branches of the redwoods, and bounces and dances off the water in the creek as it riffles by. Somewhere down in the canyon, a Pacific wren breaks into song. The world seems perfect just beyond Maddy's deck.

||

How come I didn't come live with you after Mom died?" We're in Maddy's kitchen. I'm making us sandwiches.

Maddy sits at the dinette. The effort it took to come find me shows on her face. "Believe me, I offered," she says. "But I was having some health issues of my own back then, and your mom and I were both worried I might not be around long enough to see you through until you were old enough to take care of yourself."

I take out three pieces of bread—two for me, one for Maddy—put the bread wrapper to my lips, suck the air out, spin it, and put the twist tie back on. Maddy says exposure to air makes bread get stale faster. "Are you better?"

"Yes and no. It's a progressive disease, but it's under control."

"You're my best friend. You can't ever die."

She laughs. "Don't wish that on me. And you're my best friend, too, Finch. There's no one in the world I love more than I love you. Did you know that?"

"What about those kids in the photo album?" I rummage in the utensil drawer for the carrot scraper.

"My niece and nephew?"

"Don't you love them?"

"I used to. Very much," Maddy says.

"How come you stopped?" I hold up a bag of spinach. She nods.

"I didn't stop. I just couldn't keep my heart split open forever hoping for a relationship. I was like you with your father. You can't go on loving someone who is never going to love you back. It wasn't their fault. It was my mother's. After a while I had to let them go. Close the book."

"What did your mother do?"

"Not much mayonnaise on mine."

"Stop watching me. I know how you like it." I put the mayo back in the fridge. "So, your mother?"

"She was a bit like your dad, I guess."

"An awful person?" I try to smile.

"No." Then she gets that I am trying to lighten up. Her smile is thin and strained. "She just didn't have a heart big enough for me. Family dynamics are a mystery, Finch. And what people are capable and incapable of is a bigger mystery. Do you remember when I said a good way to judge people is to see what they can turn their backs on?"

"I think so."

"It was the day you brought me the bird that hit your window."

"The finch."

"That's right. I said you were a good person and you said anybody would have done the same thing."

"I remember." I put the carrot peels in the compost bucket.

"Your father was who I was thinking of when I said that. Your father, my sister, my mother, and the people who owned that dog." Maddy nods toward the dog, who's lying on the deck watching us through the front window.

"Did your mother leave you?"

"Not physically. She deserted me emotionally."

"What does that mean?"

Maddy's lips compress. "If she ever loved me, she got over it."

I glance at the dog and think of Otus and Rav—and me. No wonder Maddy takes in things that need love. "Did she tell you she didn't love you anymore?"

"No. She showed me."

"How?"

"It isn't worth talking about. It happened a long time ago." Maddy uses her cane to help her stand. "You want some juice?"

"Sit. I'll get it."

When she got up, so did the dog. She sits. He sits. Maddy looks at me and shakes her head.

"Life's pretty bad, isn't it?"

"No, honey," Maddy says. "Life isn't bad, it's tough. And, thankfully, just some of the time."

|||

carry our spinach, shredded carrot, and Swiss cheese sandwiches out to the table on the back deck. Maddy stands at the railing looking down at the creek. A raven calls. We both look up and watch it cross overhead. "Did you know I was adopted?" she says.

I put glasses on the table. "No. From foster care?"

"I don't think there was anything like foster care back then. I was born in a home for unwed mothers. Back then birth mothers were forced to keep and care for their babies for three months, then give them up for adoption after they bonded—probably as punishment for the sin of getting pregnant out of wedlock. Can you imagine?" She lowers herself into one of the plastic deck chairs. "Think how you felt about that little possum after just two days. Or how that dog mourns for his family."

Maddy never talks about herself. I stay quiet, afraid if I speak she'll change the subject.

"When my adoptive parents took me home, I was already three months old. Maybe that all-important initial bonding never happened. I don't know. They'd been told they couldn't have children but my sister was born four and a half years later."

"At least you have a sister."

"Not anymore."

"Did she die?"

"Not yet." Maddy smiles. "No, she's alive and well. Ours was a pretty dysfunctional family. My father was an alcoholic, and my mother made me her little ally. I can't count the nights she woke us, loaded us in the car, and went out looking for him—bar to bar, ditch to ditch. He seemed to be the reason she was so miserable. I grew up blaming him for her unhappiness, and for mine. I thought I hated him, so we never had any kind of relationship until the last few years of his life."

A late-season yellow jacket lands on Maddy's glass of orange juice. We watch it cruise down the inside of the glass and drink its fill.

"Was your mom mean to you?"

"No. Not mean."

The yellow jacket is buzzing her sandwich.

"She just never let me forget a misstep." Maddy breaks off a piece of her crust and puts it on the table for the yellow jacket. "Our housekeeper once called her a grudgeful woman. Her best friend, the woman I'm named after, was a Christian Scientist. When my mother got breast cancer—"

"Your mother had breast cancer, too?"

Maddy nods. "Christian Scientists think illnesses are caused by imperfect beliefs, and that prayer heals by replacing bad thoughts with good ones. Because of her religion, her best friend wouldn't acknowledge Mom's cancer, and my mother never spoke to her again. They'd been friends for seventy-four years."

"How come you never had children?"

Rufus jumps up on Maddy's lap. She scratches his ear. "Mom used to say that if it weren't for us, Kristine and me, she would have left my father. I decided that if children were the net women got tangled in, I would never have any."

"But you liked your niece and nephew?"

Maddy closes her eyes. "I loved them more than if they were my own. Tommy was the oldest. Before my mother died, he and I spent hours together walking in the woods, catching frogs, lizards, and bugs, and wading in the icy waters of Sanlando Springs. He loved me so much my sister wouldn't tell him I was coming to visit until I drove up the driveway, because he would sit at the window waiting for me. Noelle, my niece, was only two when Mom died."

"It's amazing that your mom died of breast cancer, too."

Maddy nods. "Metastasized to her bones just like your mom's, but at least my mother lived to be seventy-seven."

"What happened to your niece and nephew?"

"It's too long a story." Maddy waves the yellow jacket away from my orange juice.

Something in her tone makes me think she wants to tell me. "I want to hear it."

Maddy thinks about it for a moment. "Maybe it will tell you something about families and how important good ones are. When my grandmother died, my mom inherited three or four thousand acres of farmland in Iowa and Nebraska. My mother grew up privileged but until my grandmother passed, we lived comfortably but pretty bare bones compared to the way Momma was raised. That money became her safety net. She guarded it like a mongrel with a bone.

"When she died, she left it all to my sister." Maddy takes a deep breath and looks away. The Pacific wren is singing again. She closes her eyes to listen.

"I don't get it."

Maddy picks up her sandwich, but doesn't take a bite. "On one hand I can understand that she was passing the safety net on to her daughter and her daughter's children, but emotionally, it was pretty devastating. Kristine realized how hurtful what Mom did was. She cried as hard as I did, but I knew right then that my mother had blown our family to smithereens. Kristine's husband was an attorney." Maddy's tone turns sharp. "He was so eager to get his hands on Momma's will he had it delivered to the house on a Sunday—the day after she died. It didn't take him long to convince Kristine that it was fair. After all, Kristine was her only *real* daughter. I adored my niece and nephew, but after that, whatever guilt Kristine felt made me pretty unwelcome. When I tried to see the kids, she came up with excuses: dance lessons, tennis lessons, always too busy. The last time I saw either one of them was for fifteen minutes at a Dunkin' Donuts in Orlando. Shortly after that I moved here."

"I'm so sorry."

She shoos away my sympathy like the bothersome yellow jacket. "It's been twenty-five years, but it still hurts and I still miss them. Silly, huh?"

"I don't think so. I still miss my mother."

"Oh, Finch. Of course you do. It's completely different. I've spent all these years trying to figure out where I went wrong, what it was about me that made me someone my mother couldn't love equally and my sister didn't love enough to want me in her life."

"I wonder if that's how I'll feel twenty-five years from now."

Maddy frowns. "That question should never occur to you. I was asking the wrong question all along. I should have been asking what was wrong with *them*." She combs my bangs aside with her fingers.

I lean and put my arms around her shoulders. "Now you and I are family."

"You're the grandchild I never had. But more than that,

Finch, you are surrounded by people who love you. You don't have to be related by blood to be a family. Stan and Cindee—"

"They don't care about me."

"You're wrong, and one of these days, you'll realize that."

I walk up to check Maddy's mail and see the dog. He's almost to the first bend in the road and trotting along as if today will be different from yesterday. I want to shout at him, tell him he's wasting his time. No one wants him. No one is coming back to get him. Even if he could understand, he wouldn't believe me, any more than I would have believed Stan if he'd told me my father didn't want me.

The dog must sense me watching because he stops at the top of the hill and looks back.

We stare at each other.

I break off first and turn for home.

CHAPTER 25

I

I come out of the woods from Maddy's and have started across our yard when I hear a muffled voice coming from the shed. I stop and listen before tiptoeing over to flatten myself against the outside wall. I lean and peer in the cobwebby, crud-caked window, but it's too dark inside for me to see anything.

"I don't know what else to say but thank you." It's Stan's voice.

I edge along the wall to the door that's ajar. It's bright outside and it takes a moment for my eyes to adjust to the dim, cluttered interior. Stan's sitting on the lawn mower, elbows on the steering wheel, his forehead resting on laced fingers. I think he's either crying or praying. I step away so he won't catch me watching.

I was in the third grade last time I saw an adult cry. Mom always met me at the school bus stop, but she wasn't there that day. I ran to the house, remembering just in time not to let the front door bang shut. I went in quietly, and heard noises coming from the laundry room. My parents were on the floor in front of the washing machine. Dad had his arms locked in a circle around my mother, pinning her arms to her sides. Mom was sobbing, and Dad's forehead was pressed against her heaving shoulders. Clothes, towels, and sheets were everywhere, as if the laundry basket had exploded. I began to cry, too, even though I didn't know what was wrong. They lied and told me they'd had a fight, and were crying because they were sorry, but I know now it was the day Mom found out the new lump was also cancer and they were going to remove her other breast.

The shock of that memory and what it must take to make Stan cry scares me. I panic and fling open the door, filling the shed with sunlight.

Stan sits up and blinks.

"Why are you crying?"

"I'm not." His red-rimmed eyes remind me of the dog's.

"Sounds like you are."

"Allergies."

"Bull. You're not sick, are you?"

"No."

"Then what's the matter?" Another possibility occurs to me. "Are you and Cindee getting a divorce?"

"No, Morgan. It's nothing."

"I don't believe you. You wouldn't cry about nothing." My tone is demanding and I'm making him defensive. "Please," I say softly. "You're scaring me."

"Don't be scared. It's really nothing. I came in here to talk to . . . Cindee's God."

"But you don't believe in God."

"That's not true. I don't know one way or the other. A lot of people believe in him, or at least in some higher power. And in case they're right, I thought I'd try to make amends."

"What are you praying for?"

"A little forgiveness."

I doubt he means for the day he dragged me off the toilet. "What for?"

"This is between you and me, okay? You can't ever tell Cindee."

"I won't. I promise."

He doesn't say anything for a few seconds. "If you get mad at her and use this to hurt her—"

I step inside the shed and stand in front of him. "I won't ever tell, Stan. I swear on Mom's memory."

His face sags. Tears swim in his eyes.

I put my hand on his arm. "Is it about Mom?"

"Cindee's being sick brought your mom's illness back. I suddenly missed her so much I couldn't bear it. I've never loved anyone the way I loved your mother—and I never will again."

Relief fills my chest. "I always thought—"

"That I married Cindee too soon after your mom died?"

I nod.

"I married her because she was kind and caring, and I needed someone to help me raise you. I thought I was being fair to your mom because I didn't love Cindee, and she knew it. She said it didn't matter. We liked each other and that was a good place to start. The thing is, when she got sick last week, I realized I do love her."

I move my hand up to his shoulder. "She's not going to die, is she?"

"No. No. It was just a bad cold, but it made me realize I'm happy with her. Your mom brought us together. She picked me so you'd have a dad, and I picked Cindee so you'd have a mom."

I want to hug him and I think he wants to hug me, but neither of us moves.

Stan looks past me and clears his throat. "There's your buddy."

I turn. The dog's at the end of the driveway, watching us. I put an arm around Stan's neck and my head on his shoulder. "Maddy told me Mom was the happiest she'd ever seen her when she was married to you."

His breath catches. "Oh, Morgan . . . sorry, Finch . . . you can't imagine what that means to me."

II

Later that afternoon, after Maddy feeds the dog, I give him plenty of time to get home before I follow. I dismount at the bottom of the dirt drive and push my bike far enough up the hill to hide it from the road. I prop it against a tree and silently climb the rest of the way.

The dog's asleep in a bare dirt hollow under the same tree they tied him to before driving away. The rope they used is still around it, though it has stiffened and turned black. A week ago, I wondered how he could be stupid enough to cling to this place and to the people who left him to starve. Now I know.

He's dreaming. His legs twitch and he's making little barking sounds. I watch and imagine he's chasing his people down the road. In his mind, this time they stop and come back for him. It helps to make up something to hope for, the way I made up what I wanted my father to be.

I stand watching his sides rise and fall, waiting for him to wake. I don't wait long. The dog stretches all four legs stiffly and opens his eyes. One moment, he's lying down, and the next he's on his feet and running. He crosses the open space between the tree and where the trailer was, ears pinned, tail tucked.

There's a blue plastic chair on its side. It's missing two of its three back slats. I right it and sit down. The dog paces, back and forth, watching me and eventually sits, then finally lies down, paws together.

"I'm your friend, you know."

He sits up, as if my words might trap him. When I don't say anything more, he lies back down.

Something is different from the last time I was here. Things are missing from the fire ring where I found the burned remains of his collar. All that's left are the charred ends of a couple of logs, lots of cigarette butts, a few crumpled Budweiser beer cans—the same brand my father used to drink—and a wad of tinfoil. I can't remember exactly what was there before.

I glance at the sand-filled tractor tire. There'd been a doll partly buried there, but it's gone, too. For a moment, I wonder if his family came back for some of the things they left behind—except the dog.

There's a pile of junk under the bull pine I don't remember from last time. I get up, which startles the dog. He leaps sideways and begins to pace. I ignore him and walk over to the tree, squat, and push aside a tricycle tire.

Beneath it is the armless doll. There's a pink plastic hairbrush and matching comb with most of the teeth missing, a tennis ball with one side blown out, a baby's rattle, a diaper, now home to a banana slug, and a red plastic dog's dish.

He's collected the few things his family left behind. This pile of trash is *his* keepsakes.

I can again feel the cold wind battering my hand as I

watch my keepsakes fly out of the flapping Crown Royal bag. "They aren't coming back for you." My tears blur the dog. "No one is coming back for either of us."

The dog lies down with his head on his paws, brow furrowed, but sits up when I wipe my eyes on my sleeve and go back to the broken chair. The charred piece of his collar is in the pocket of my hoodie. I take it out and open my palm. "Do you want this for your collection—" I look at the *B-E*. "—Ben?"

The dog's ears rise in recognition.

"Ben is your name, isn't it?" I toss the collar onto his pile.

He makes a wide arc around where I sit, goes over to sniff his collar, looks at me, and lies down beside his stash.

I slip out of the chair to sit on the ground. After a moment, I lean a little forward and put my hand out to him. He looks at it, then at me. Not the usual way he side-eyes me, with a crescent of white showing, but straight into my eyes. Neither of us moves.

My stomach muscles begin to quiver from the strain of holding out my arm. I'm about to lower it when Ben inches a paw forward. I put my hand on the ground and slide it forward until there are only inches between my fingertips and his paw.

"I'm your friend, Ben," I whisper, and close my eyes. I don't open them, even when I hear him sniffing and feel the grit his exhalations blow over my fingers. I hold still until his cold, wet nose touches my hand.

I open my eyes. His head is on the ground and he's looking up at me. I lift a finger and touch his nose. His skin quivers, but he doesn't move.

My back aches from holding this position. I sit up slowly. Ben does, too, but he doesn't run. I arch my back and rotate my shoulders. When the ache goes away, I reach out to him again. He extends his neck and sniffs my fingertips, then lies down, feet together. I run my fingers across his toes. He watches for a moment then rolls on his side.

A lump forms in my throat. I stroke his face, rub an ear, and run my hand down his neck to the rope. It's tight. I'll need both hands to work the knots loose.

"Will you let me take this off?"

His ears twitch but he lies still. I begin to pick at the first of the two knots with just one finger. His eyes roll to watch when I bring my other hand up. He tenses, putting all his effort into lying still.

"I'll get you a new collar with your name on it. And you can sleep in my room where it's dry and warm."

The first knot comes undone and I feed the chewed, frayed end of the rope through and begin working on the second one. When he closes his eyes, my heart nearly bursts.

The second knot is tighter than the first, so tight it's hard to get a finger between it and his skin. I break two nails, one to the quick, but I keep plucking at it. "I don't know, Ben. I think I need a knife for this one."

He lifts his head to look at me, puts a paw on my knee, and lies back down.

I work a bit longer, pulling frayed strands of the rope through until I'm finally able to untie it. The loop of rope is buried so deep that it looks like his skin has begun to grow over it. As gently as I can, I pull it loose, leaving a hairless furrow and a bloody sore where it was knotted. I turn and pitch the length of rope. It lands with the junk from his past.

When I get up, Ben scrambles to his feet and shakes, creating a cloud of dust.

"Let's go home." I walk toward where I left my bike. When I look back, Ben sits watching me. "Come on." I pat my thigh.

He comes and licks my hand. I squat down in front of him and put an arm across his shoulders. He licks my ear.

I start down the hill again, but he turns and runs to the pile of mementos, picks up something, and trots to catch up. It's the ruptured tennis ball. When he's beside me, he puts it on the ground, pushes it toward me with his nose, and backs up. I pick it up and throw it as hard as I can. Ben races after it, brings it back, puts it at my feet, and dances backward, tail wagging, wearing a dog smile.

|||

Maddy's taking a sack of groceries from her car as Ben and I come down the driveway. She turns when she hears my brakes squeal, gasps, and puts her hand to her heart. "Lord love a duck."

I grin.

"And you got the rope off. How in the world?"

I shrug. "I think Ben—his name *is* Ben—wanted us to be friends as much as I did. He just needed to get past being afraid."

Maddy puts the sack of groceries back in the hatchback and sits beside the bag. She holds her hand out to Ben. He wags his tail but doesn't move. I lean my bike against the deck railing and go to sit beside Maddy. She puts her arm around me. "Not many people would have the patience it took, Finch. You've done a good thing."

"Anyone would have—" I hold my hand up to keep her from reminding me to judge people by what they can turn their backs on. "Never mind."

Ben has found a stick. He trots back with it in his mouth, drops it at Maddy's feet, and dances backward. She leans to pick it up but can't bend over that far. Before I can get it for her, Ben picks it up and puts it in her lap. She throws it as hard as she can, then turns to me and tries to say something but ends up fanning back tears with her hand.

We watch him race across the yard, skid past where the stick landed, turn, leap on it, and start back to us.

"There's a lesson in this." Maddy pats my knee.

"Of course there is." I laugh, and lean to bump her shoulder with mine.

"Not just for you, smarty-pants. For both of us."

"Like what?" Ben's back with the stick.

"It's a Native American allegory about the secret to being happy. Old goat that I am, I can't remember how it goes exactly, but it's a tale of a battle between two wolves."

I throw the stick for Ben, hard enough that it lands above his head in the low-hanging branches of the plum tree. "Go on."

"One wolf embodies despair and darkness—like the anger you feel toward your father and the sorrow and resentment I feel toward my mother and my sister—" She holds out one hand palm up. "—and the other wolf is forgiveness and love." She turns her other palm up.

Ben stares up at the stick, whines, then barks at it, tail wagging.

"Which one wins?"

"The one you feed."

I lean my head against Maddy's shoulder.

She pats my cheek.

CHAPTER 26

1

As far as I know, Ben never went back to his old place. He still goes to Maddy's for his two meals a day, waits for me after school next to Maddy's mailbox, and follows me everywhere when I'm home.

Cindee said it was okay for Ben to sleep in my room, but he's wary of Stan and runs from him. I've tried to lure him into the house on Stan and Cindee's date night, but he won't cross the threshold. For now, he sleeps in Maddy's carport on the dog bed she bought him.

The first thing Stan asked when I told him Ben was now my dog was who's going to be responsible if he needs a vet.

"I will, of course," Maddy says when I tell her what Stan said. "I'm the one who encouraged him to stick around. He's my responsibility." I'm holding Ben's head still while she applies Neosporin to the still-raw rope burn on the back of his neck. "And when he trusts us enough, I'll take him in for his shots and to be neutered."

II

Cindee and I are at Harvest Market. She's in produce and I'm in dairy getting eggs and butter. I'm trying to decide which brand of cage-free eggs to buy—organic or not. Cindee always gets the white ones because they're four dollars less a dozen, but Mom told me they come from chickens that are forced to live in cages and are pumped full of hormones and antibiotics.

There's a woman standing in front of the refrigerated pies. Out of the corner of my eye, I see her watching me. More than watching, she's staring, and there is something familiar-looking about her. Maybe she's a friend of my mother's who hasn't seen me since the funeral. I don't want to be rude, so I smile, but she's looking at my hair and then she looks directly at my crotch. I look down, too. I'm wearing leggings, my light blue high-top All Stars, a short denim skirt, and a light blue hoodie that matches my eyes. The skirt isn't tight so nothing shows down there.

Our eyes meet. Hers are not friendly. "You're Morgan."

Before I can answer, I see Amanda coming up behind her carrying a jar of peanut butter. She's grinning like she's been handed the keys to a new car. Now I know why the woman looks familiar. She's an older, wrinkled version of her daughter.

"Hey, Morgan." Amanda puts the peanut butter in their cart. "Like your hair."

"Hey," I mutter, thinking she'll be nice in front of her mother.

"Mom, this is the *girl*—" She smirks and makes air quotes with her fingers. "—I told you about."

"At least your parents made you cut your hair," Mrs. Ellis says. She takes a cream pie out of the refrigerator and puts it into her cart with the peanut butter. "I've told Amanda she should feel sorry for you, didn't I, dear? You have a mental disorder that needs professional treatment. It's nothing to laugh about."

Amanda's nose crinkles when she grins, but her eyes don't thaw.

The lid is up on the brand of eggs I'd chosen. I was making sure none were cracked. Whatever I might say refuses to form in my mind. I look at Amanda's mother.

Her upper lip curls in disgust, and the resemblance to Amanda gets stronger. "What are your parents thinking letting you dress like a girl?"

"Because I am a girl."

She turns her cart so she can lean closer. "You've got boy parts, you're a boy." Little drops of spittle fly out with her words. "Pretending to be a girl is sick." Her voice is now loud enough to stop other shoppers and bring the bakery people to the counter. Even Amanda seems surprised by the force of her mother's anger.

"Mom." She puts her hand on her mother's arm. "People are listening."

"Let them. There's a pervert in the making here. Everyone should know."

Someone has come to stand beside me. I glance to my left. It's Cindee. "What's going on here?" she demands.

"This *boy* is pretending to be a girl."

Cindee gasps. "How dare you!" She steps between me and Mrs. Ellis and begins to rummage in her purse for her cell phone. She finds it and shakes it at Amanda's mother. "One more word out of you and I'm calling the police. You are verbally abusing a child and I *will* press charges."

Other shoppers have stopped to stare.

"What kind of mother lets her son take hormones and be surgically—you know?"

Cindee looks at me. I see her mind trying to sort this out, then she blinks and turns back to Mrs. Ellis. "Those decisions for my . . . my daughter are years away. Right now, it's about clothes, hairstyles, and pronouns." Cindee leans close to Mrs. Ellis's face. "So back the hell off."

Amanda's mother swings her cart between herself and Cindee. "God help you both."

"You're the one in need of help, lady." Cindee takes the carton of eggs out of my hand and closes the lid. "You're a hater, and you're grooming your daughter to be one, too." Cindee puts the eggs in our cart, then points a finger at Amanda's mother. "If you or your kid ever so much as look cross-eyed at Finch again, I'll take it up with our attorney and with the school board."

There comes a smattering of applause from the small crowd, and one of the ladies behind the bakery counter gives me a thumbs-up.

Like that, it's over. Amanda and her mother steer around us down the aisle past the cookies.

The trembling starts in my stomach, and spreads. Soon I'm shaking so hard I grab the edge of the butter shelf to keep from falling. All I can think of is, where did this person who looks just like Cindee come from?

"We should always buy cage-free eggs." Cindee puts her arm around my waist.

————

During our slow, abundance-of-caution drive home, I keep looking at her, like she's going to turn back into the woman who wanted to send me to Jesus camp.

"What?" she says.

"You stood up for me." *You even called me your daughter.*

Cindee turns on her signal and pulls into the Humane Society's thrift shop parking lot. She shifts into park and turns to face me.

"This may sound over the top, but I personally felt the pain she was inflicting." She makes a fist and mock stabs herself in the heart.

"What do you mean?"

She faces forward and puts her hands together at the top of the steering wheel. "I have to be honest, Mor . . . Finch. I used to feel sorry for you." She lifts her head and looks at me. "I thought this I'm-a-girl thing was because your mom died. I tried to be compassionate." She begins to slide her cross along its chain. It makes a little zipping sound. "But to hear that woman spew such hatred . . ."

I'm still shaken by what happened and don't think I can stand a sermon right now. I put my left thumb on the seat belt release and move my right hand to the door handle.

"I'm not a very smart person," Cindee says.

I bring my hands together in my lap. "You're smart." I try to sound like I mean it.

"No." She shakes her head, her lips compressed. "I don't have an education. I watch too much junk on TV. I read those stupid tabloids."

"That doesn't mean you're not smart."

"What I'm trying to say is, I may have let my beliefs get

in the way of accepting that you have been telling the truth. This might be hard for you to believe, but I love you and I don't want you hurt."

I look down at my hands in my lap and turn them palms up.

"A few days ago, I got on the computer and typed—" She lets go of the cross and air types. "—'my son thinks he's a girl.'" She glances at me, then away. "You're transgender."

My stomach feels full of feathers. "I know."

She goes back to zipping her cross along its chain. "It said, your gender identity is between your ears—what you are in your head and your heart. What sex you are"—a blush travels up her neck to her whole face—"is between your legs." She reaches and takes my hand. "In your case, they don't match. I printed everything out for you and made Stan read it, too. I'm sorry I didn't try to find out what was going on earlier."

I nod, but think of Ben. I could have tried harder to find his truth.

Cindee forgets she didn't turn the engine off, but before I can stop her, she turns the key and the starter grinds. "Oops." She laughs and pats my knee, then her smile fades.

"One more thing, Finch. You're going to have a difficult time. Many people will be nice and accepting, but others are going to be like Amanda and her mother. Those wounds can cut deep."

"Wounds heal." I try to sound unconcerned when I'm really scared that there will be more times like today.

"They do. Just try not to let the haters leave the deeper marks."

Amanda's the only hater I know. I'll never let her scar me, but it makes me wonder about Ben. Even after his wound heals, how long will it take that scar to fade? Or will it ever?

CHAPTER 27

I

On a Saturday near the middle of January, Sherri shows up at my door crying so hard she has the hiccups. "Mom and Jake broke up. For good this time."

I'm not surprised. She told me a couple weeks ago they'd been fighting constantly since they came back unmarried from Las Vegas. "I'm sorry, but—"

Cindee's showering and I assume Stan is, as usual, up a tree. When I hear the water go off and the swish of the shower curtain, I step outside and close the door. "Is that a bad thing?"

"Hell yes. He was paying the rent and he moved out yesterday. Mom had to give our landlord notice. The next week is paid for, then she'll use whatever we get back from the cleaning deposit to move somewhere else."

Stan comes out of the woodshed and waves.

We wave back. "We can't talk here," I say. "Let's go down to the creek."

On the way, Sherri tells me her mother was sure Jake would marry her while they were in Las Vegas, the quickie-marriage capital of the world, but he didn't.

"Mom always does this. Gets her hopes up, ends up disappointed, gets mad, and burns the relationship. Deanne and I like Jake. Some of Mom's boyfriends have been much worse."

"There must be single men here. Mom found Stan, and so did Cindee."

"That should tell you something. The only single man got recycled. Even if she met someone, I don't think there's enough time to hook him into paying the bills." Sherri looks up at the trees. "It's pretty here."

We sit on my redwood bridge, dangling our legs off the side. We've had enough rain to fill the creek and make the waterfall loud.

I practically have to shout, "My mom's ashes are between those two trees."

"Wow." Sherri squints and stares at where I pointed.

I elbow her. "They're not still there."

"Of course." A hint of color creeps into her cheeks. She looks down at the rushing water and swings her feet. "It's a nice spot."

We sit for a few minutes watching the water tumble by, and it finally sinks in, my second best friend in the world is going to leave. I take her hand. "Where will you go?"

Sherri shrugs. "I don't know. Mom's been online sending out ten-year-old pictures of herself. She's met a guy who lives in Portland and another in Seattle. I guess we'll head north." Sherri squeezes my hand. "Do you think your stepparents would let me stay with you for a while?"

"Wow. Maybe. I don't know." My mind races. "We could ask. That would be so much fun. How long is a while?"

"Till school's out?"

It's mid-January. "You mean until school's out in June?"

She picks at a drop of sap on her jeans rather than look at me. "Yeah."

"Oh." I try to imagine Stan's reaction. "I don't know. Our house is only two bedrooms, and I have a twin bed."

"Mom will buy me a bed. It's the least she can do."

"What about Deanne? What's she going to do?"

"Will's mom said she could stay there till school's out."

Now I know this was a plan she and Deanne cooked up, but I don't care. My best friend, besides Maddy, living with us would be like having a sister. "Is Will out of jail?"

"No. He's in juvie for another six months at least."

"And your mom's okay with that?"

Tears swim in Sherri's eyes. "It was her idea. It will be easier to land a new 'fish'"—she makes air quotes—"if we stay here until she's settled somewhere."

I can't help but think that if Sherri's mom leaves without her and Deanne, she'll never send for them. That worry must show in my eyes.

"Mom's *not* like your father, Finch. She won't desert us."

"I know," I say, though I don't. "We'll have to ask Cindee, and she'll have to ask Stan."

Sherri hugs me and jumps up. "Let's go." She pulls me across the redwood bridge.

Ben barks and I glance up. He and Maddy are looking down on us from her deck. Maddy waves. Ben's head is cocked to one side like he's worried Sherri's hurting me.

"Hi, Maddy." I wave.

"Who's that with you?"

"My friend Sherri."

"Nice to meet you."

"You, too," Sherri says, though probably not loud enough for Maddy to hear.

Maddy watches us cross the tree to the other bank. "You girls looked upset. Is everything okay?"

"Yeah," I say, but can see by the expression on Maddy's face that she's suspicious.

"Why don't you two come up for some juice?"

"Can't right now, Maddy."

Sherri says, "I have to be going."

"Some other time, then." We climb the hill, and Maddy is still watching when I turn to wave before entering the trail through the woods.

Cindee's in the kitchen making sandwiches. Her hair is wrapped in a towel. "I'm happy to finally meet you," Sherri says when I introduce them. She crosses the kitchen and shakes Cindee's hand.

Screaming family members are jumping up and down and hugging each other on *Family Feud.* "I love that show," Sherri says. "My mom said when my sister and I are older maybe we can try out." She looks at the TV. "It'll never happen. There are only three of us."

"It's not fair, is it?" Cindee sets the DVR to record the rest of the show and turns the set off. "My husband and Finch are all there is of our family, too."

I square my shoulders and take a breath. "We have a favor to ask."

Cindee smiles.

"Sherri's mom . . . needs to find another—"

"Job," Sherri blurts, afraid, I guess, that I was going to say "man." "She's got a lead on one in Seattle, so Finch and I were wondering if I could stay here—" She pauses. "—

so I don't have to miss any school when she goes for the interview."

Cindee glances at me.

I hold up crossed fingers on both hands.

"I don't see why not," Cindee says. "But I'll have to ask my husband. The only problem I can see is that there's only one bed in Finch's room."

"I've got a sleeping bag," Sherri offers, "or maybe my mother could rent a rollaway from the Rent-All place."

"That would work." Cindee smiles at me once more.

It's good that Sherri's making it sound like a few days to Cindee, when it could turn into weeks, and weeks into months. Better to see what happens than to worry about how long.

"Shall I call your mom?" Cindee says.

Now Sherri glances at me. "I'd better ask her first. If she agrees, could I have her call you?"

"Sure, and that will give me time to clear it with Stan."

Sherri and I wait until we're at the end of the driveway before starting to laugh and hug each other. I watch until she's out of sight, then run down the road to Maddy's. Ben is sitting by her mailbox. He jumps up, tail wagging, picks up the stick he was chewing, and trots beside me down the driveway.

CHAPTER 28

I

"Tell your parents the truth and let them handle it,"
Maddy says when I tell her about Sherri moving in.
She's using the garden hose to wash out the can she
keeps on the counter next to the sink for the kitchen
scraps she composts.

My parents? I feel a jolt. "They're *not* my parents."

"Yes, they are, Finch. You don't have to give birth to a
child to parent it."

"Sherri is my best friend. She and her sister drove me
to Eureka."

"Which they shouldn't have done, but that's not the
point." She sniffs the can and wrinkles her nose. "You two
have led Cindee to believe this is just for a few days. You
have to tell them the truth. Maybe they'll say okay, but I
doubt it."

Ben drops the chewed-up stick at my feet. I kick it away.

Maddy scowls, picks it up, and throws it for him. She
turns back to me. "Let's go back to the parent thing. You
know how solicitous Cindee is of Stan?"

"She's ridiculous." Ben returns with the stick, drops it
at my feet, and does his happy-dog dance.

"That's because she loves him more than he loves her."

"He loves her. He told me so."

"I'm glad to hear that, but it wasn't true in the beginning. That man loved your mother like nothing I've ever seen. He may not be perfect—"

"By a long shot." I don't know why I'm acting like this.

"Finch, that's enough. Sit down and shut up."

Maddy's never raised her voice before. I sit on the top step next to the compost bin.

"After your trip to Eureka, you must realize it takes a pretty special man to marry a woman with a kid, a kid he may have to raise if her cancer comes back. Stan's got rough edges, but he's a kind man, and he made your mother very happy for the cancer-free year they had together.

"That would have been enough, but he turned out to be one in a million. That said, your mom knew who you were, your true self, her daughter, and knew that Stan thought she coddled you. She worried that after she was gone, he'd be harder on you. Stan has physical custody of you but I've been your legal guardian since your father left."

Maddy made a hole in the compost pile to dump in the fresh scraps. I'm watching the exposed earthworms burrowing their way back underground when she says this. I look up. "What does that mean?"

"It means you live with Stan and he can make decisions about how to raise you, but I'm your permanent legal guardian. In other words, I have the final say."

My mind reels. All this time, Maddy could have been raising me. I can't catch my breath. "Why didn't you tell me?"

"Because you would have felt free to act exactly as you are acting now. I'm meant to be your backup."

"If he loved Mom like you say, why'd he marry Cindee so quick after she died?" I know the answer, but never told Maddy what Stan told me. I'm not sure why. Maybe because I was afraid if she knew things have gotten better at home, she'd stop worrying about me.

She's using a pitchfork to cover the new food scraps with a fresh layer of grass clippings and leaves.

"Your mom wanted you to have a family, Finch." She straightens and rubs her back. "He married her because he needed help raising you. He promised your mother he'd take care of you. You don't remember this, but you were blind with grief, and gave that poor man a pretty hard time. Cindee was the hospice volunteer who came to help Stan with your mom."

I get up, take the pitchfork, and finish covering the new scraps. "I only remember her coming once or twice."

"She came when you were at school." Maddy takes my place on the steps. "Your mom wanted your life to be as normal as possible. I think that's the reason her dying was such a shock to you. She put on a brave front when you were in the house."

I toss the stick for Ben again and take a seat on the step below Maddy's.

"Cindee was wonderful to your mom," Maddy says. "She's a kind person, and Stan was right up front with her—told her he needed help with you and told her he'd treat her right if she married him."

A banana slug, eyeballs on stalks, is gliding toward me. "Why couldn't he have just paid her to take care of me?" I tap it with a redwood leaf to watch it retract its eyes.

"He wanted you to grow up as part of a family. A single man trying to raise a kid who's not his own, with a pretty young woman hired to help out was not the picture he wanted you to live with. He created a family for you out of his determination to honor your mother."

I feel myself deflate. "But Sherri's my only other friend besides you."

Maddy lifts my chin. "I know you think that now, but you'll make other friends. Either way, you have to be honest. Tell them the truth, and let them decide if they want, or can even afford, another mouth to feed for heaven knows how long."

"Her mom will send money."

"Tell them the truth."

CHAPTER 29

1

Sherri called me after Stan talked to her mother to say they were moving to Portland. That was a week ago. She didn't come back to school or return any of my calls. Today is the day they're leaving and she still hasn't called to say goodbye. Twice I pick up the phone and stand there with it until the dial tone is replaced by the high-pitched disconnect alert. The third time, I swallow my pride, punch in her number, and hear, "This number is no longer in service."

There's no way Sherri could have known I told Stan and Cindee the truth—that her mother wasn't going for an interview, she was leaving for good. How Stan handled it impressed me. He made it seem like discovering the truth was accidental. He called using the speakerphone, and when her mother answered, he said how pleased they were to have Sherri stay with them while she went for a job interview.

"What interview?" her mother said. "I got no interview; I got no job; I got nothing."

"I'm very sorry," Stan said, cool as could be. "I guess my wife misunderstood. Well, we wish you all the best."

There was silence on the other end for a moment. "Thanks."

"Who's that?" It was Sherri's voice.

"Your friend's father. What'd you tell them?"

Stan put his hand on my shoulder.

"Hang up," Sherri said.

The voices are muffled for a minute, like her mother covered the receiver with her hand, then Sherri screamed, "You're ruining my life!" and the line went dead.

About one o'clock, I give up on Sherri's coming to say goodbye and walk with Ben to Maddy's.

"Did she call?" Maddy is putting a bar of suet in the feeder. Otus, in his cage on the hill, hears her voice and starts to trill.

I shake my head.

"Don't feel too bad, honey." She puts an arm around my shoulder and kisses my cheek. "You'll make other friends."

"I don't know, Maddy."

"Why do you say that? Of course you will."

We're putting sunflower seeds into the other feeder when Ben jumps up, runs across the yard, and disappears in the woods. I look up. The red Mustang, with a U-Haul trailer attached, pulls over at the top of the driveway. Sherri jumps out. I run to meet her. We hug and start to cry.

"I'm sorry," we both say at the same time. "Why?" we say.

"I told Stan you wanted to live with us until June."

"It doesn't matter. It was a dumb plan."

Over Sherri's shoulder, I see Deanne in the passenger seat.

"Deanne's going with you?"

"That didn't work out, either. Will's mother's a real piece of work."

Sherri's mom beeps the horn. We hug again.

"Promise you'll write," I say.

"I promise. Mom says she loves it here, so maybe we'll move back someday."

We drape our arms over each other's shoulders, and walk up the driveway.

After they drive away, I feel so empty.

CHAPTER 30

On a Monday, three weeks after Sherri left, I step off the school bus and look for Ben. I whistle and call him. Nothing.

I hear boys shouting and laughing, then the sound of skateboard wheels on pavement. Three boys come flying down the hill. No wonder Ben is missing. I watch them, smiling. It looks like fun, but scary.

From the other direction, a car is coming. Between their whoops and the noise their skateboard wheels make, I'm not sure they hear it. I step out on the road and wave my arms. "Car coming!" I shout.

The boys see me but only the youngest one veers out of the way. The other two split up, forcing the car, which barely had time to slow down, to drive between them. The driver blasts his horn. The oldest boy shoots him a bird.

They hop off their boards nearly opposite me. The two older boys laugh and high-five each other.

"Hey, I know you," the youngest kid says.

He looks familiar, too. Then I remember. Halloween. My heart thuds in my chest. He's Sammy's cousin, Jacob.

Now he remembers. I see it in his eyes. "You were Sammy's friend. Hey, you guys, come here!" he shouts over his shoulder, then grins at me. "I got somebody I want you to meet."

They've started back up the hill for another run. "Who cares," the older one hollers.

Jacob watches me as I try to decide which direction to run. He holds his arms out like a guard in a basketball game. "Don't you want to meet a boy who thinks he's a girl?"

The boys stop and turn.

Blood whooshes in my ears. I step left and Jacob blocks me. I fake right and dodge to the left. He catches me by my sweatshirt hood and jerks me backward. My feet fly out from under me and I go down. The other two boys each pin an arm. "Pretty, ain't he?" The oldest one laughs. "Hold him down."

I kick until the oldest boy sits on my legs. I try to scream, but Jacob puts his hand over my mouth. I pray for a car to come, or for Maddy to see them from her window.

"We ain't gonna hurt you," the older boy says. "We're just checking on which parts you got and which ones you ain't got." He unzips my sweatshirt and presses his hands to my chest. "Ain't got no boobs." He grins at me, then reaches down and puts his hand under my skirt, and claws at the waistband of my leggings.

I squeeze my thighs together as tight as I can and twist my head from side to side, trying to get free of Jacob's hand. Out of the corner of my eye, I see Ben racing up the driveway. Jacob sees him, too, and screams. Ben is on the older boy, snarling and tearing at his jacket. The third boy jumps up. He grabs his skateboard, but before he can swing it at Ben's head, I'm on my feet. I leap on his back and grab him around the neck. Ben lets go of the first boy and attacks the one I'm wrestling. The oldest boy and Jacob run. I pull Ben off the one left behind. He scrambles to his feet and runs after the other two.

I sink to my knees, wrap my arms around Ben's neck, and bury my face in his neck.

CHAPTER 31

I

'm afraid to go home or to Maddy's. They'll know right away what happened. My back is covered in dust, both elbows are bloody, and my leggings are torn at the waistband.

Ben and I cut through the woods between Maddy's house and mine and take the long way around to my redwood nest by the waterfall. I curl into a ball and cry until I'm wrung out. Ben licks my arms and the back of my neck.

II

t's late afternoon and getting cold when Maddy comes to her deck railing. "Finch, are you okay? Cindee called looking for you."

Ben and I climb the hill.

Her brow creases when she sees me. "Did you fall?"

I shake my head.

"What happened?"

Before I can stop them, tears spill down my cheeks.

Maddy figures it out and cups my face between her hands. "Who did this?"

"Some boys."

"Damn it." Maddy wipes my tears with her thumbs, hugs me so tightly it hurts, then marches me into the house, calls the sheriff, then Stan and Cindee.

Cindee's at the door in minutes, but Stan risks losing his license forever by driving the truck out to look for the boys. It's been over an hour so, luckily, he doesn't find them. Stan, when he's mad, can be pretty scary. Considering *how* I know this about him, I'm surprised and moved that he was angry enough to try.

The sheriff arrives as Stan is pulling into the driveway. He ignores the fact Stan was driving. They shake hands, and he accepts Maddy's invitation to come in for coffee while he questions me. I'm only able to give the sheriff Jacob's first name, a description of the other two, and the direction they ran after Ben rescued me. Not much.

III

Cindee lets me stay home from school for a couple days. I've got a black eye and bruises and scratches everywhere. I don't remember getting hit in the eye.

The sheriff stops by on Wednesday to give us good news and bad news. They caught the two older boys. Am I willing to testify? Stan and Cindee both say yes.

"What's the bad news?" I ask.

"Their parents say, if you let this drop, they won't bring charges against you."

"For what?" Stan snaps.

"Your dog bit one of the boys."

"He was protecting me."

"I know, but they can still sue. They will lose in court, but you'll have to hire a lawyer to fight it." Cindee and Stan look at each other, then at me. "I'm sorry, Finch," Cindee says. "We can't afford to do that."

On Thursday morning before school, Cindee tries to cover my black eye with some of her makeup. My skin is darker than hers. Her "peaches and cream" concealer turns my eye from black to blue-gray.

Worse, the fifth line down in the Sheriff's Log section of the Thursday afternoon paper reads, "In the 15000 block of McDowell Creek, assault on a minor." They might as well have put my address. Maddy's house and ours are the only two in the 15000 block of McDowell Creek. By Friday, everyone at school knows just enough to figure out the rest.

Amanda hasn't been in my face since her mother and Cindee got into it at the grocery store. I thought Cindee's threat to go to the school board worked. But today, Amanda keeps looking at me in math class, covering her mouth with her hand, and whispering to Lacey. After the bell rings, they're waiting for me in the hallway.

Lacey says, "What happened to your eye, Morgan?"

"Got your eye shadow on upside down." Amanda laughs.

I keep walking toward the cafeteria. They follow so close Amanda steps on one of my heels, and my shoe comes off. She kicks it away.

I turn to face them. "Back off, Amanda or . . ."

"Or what? You gonna tell your stepmother?" Her eyes shift past me. She straightens and smiles sweetly.

Lacey giggles. "There's your boyfriend."

A crowd of boys comes out of the boys' restroom, Gabe among them. He picks up my shoe on his way toward us.

Amanda gives Lacey a dirty look and flips her hair. "Hey, Gabe, I was just telling Morgan how sorry I am about what happened to . . . *her.*"

Lacey giggles again.

Gabe hands me my shoe. He either ignores or didn't notice the stress Amanda put on the pronoun. "What happened?"

"Nothing." My heart races and my chest hurts so much I think I'm having some kind of attack.

"Some high school boys attacked her." Amanda lowers her voice like she's selectively sharing my dark secret. "'Cause she's really a boy."

Gabe looks surprised. "Are you?"

I'm feeling dizzy and can't find my voice. "A girl," I finally croak.

Balled fists on her hips, face so close to mine I can smell her gum breath, Amanda says, "You are not. Everybody knows you're a boy. That's why you got beat up." She has backed me against the wall between two classrooms. The three of them form a semicircle around me.

My hands have gone numb and I feel like I might faint.

Amanda's eyes sparkle with cruel delight. Lacey's smiling but her eyes are as dull as her mind. Gabe is a few inches taller than I am. My eyes lock on his face because his eyes are curious, not mean. He looks at me for what feels like a long time. I don't know what's going to happen, or what he's thinking when he turns to Amanda. "Why do you care?"

"I—I," Amanda stammers. "My mom says he's a freak."

"You and your mother should mind your own business."

"Oh my God!" Amanda cries. "What *is* your story?"

Gabe leans his face close to hers. "What's yours?"

"I hate you both." She grabs Lacey's hand and drags her away.

Gabe smiles at me. "I'm heartbroken, aren't you?"

I can't breathe. My chest heaves as I gasp for air.

Gabe steps to one side to block Amanda's view. "You're having a panic attack," he says. "Cover your nose and mouth with both hands."

I try, but I can't lift my arms.

He hugs me and presses my nose against his shoulder. "Breathe slowly," he whispers.

Two boys run down the hall, see us, stop, then make kissing sounds and laugh.

"Look at me, not them."

I do.

"Just breathe. You're okay."

The pain in my chest eases, but I'm shivering. Gabe takes the shoe I've been holding all this time, kneels, and slips it on my foot.

"Thank you."

"Can't have you limping around with one shoe on, one shoe off."

"No, I mean you didn't have to make Amanda mad."

"Sure I did. She's a bully."

"That bully has a crush on you."

He laughs. "Bet she doesn't anymore."

I manage a weak smile. "Probably not."

"Is it true?"

By his tone, he doesn't seem to care one way or the other, but I don't answer.

"Morgan?" Gabe's still looking at me.

"I'm a girl, but—"

He nods. "You were born with boy parts?" He holds up his hand to high-five. I lay my palm against his without knowing why. "Kids like you and me have to stick together."

My skin tingles. "Like us?"

He glances toward the now-empty breezeway, then leans and puts his lips close to my ear. "I'm the *G* in LGBTQ," he whispers.

For a second, I'm not sure what he means—then I clamp my hands over my mouth to muffle my laugh of surprise. "That's so cool."

"I guess." His smile doesn't make it to his eyes. "How are you treated at home?" We're walking toward the doors to the breezeway.

"Okay."

He holds the door for me. "Just okay?"

"Mostly. How about you?"

"My mom was upset and disappointed, but she's given up trying to find a cure." His jaw muscles work, then he glances at me and smiles—a smile so full of hurt, I want to take his hand. "My father deals with it by pretending I no longer exist. We used to hang out, but not anymore."

"I'm really sorry."

He shrugs. "It is what it is."

We've reached the cafeteria. My stomach growls loudly. I blush.

He hands me a tray. "Sounds like we're here in the nick of time."

We both get chicken nuggets and fries and carry our trays to an empty table. We sit across from each other. Amanda's a few tables away, knee jiggling, staring daggers at us. I avoid making eye contact. If I look at her, I'm afraid I'll laugh out loud.

Gabe squirts a massive amount of ketchup on his plate and mixes in yellow mustard.

"What are you doing?"

He dips a fry in the concoction. "Try it."

"I don't think so."

Gabe adds a little more mustard and stirs it in with a fry. "How old are you?"

"I just turned twelve." I dip just the tip of a fry in the orange goop and touch it to my tongue. "Not bad." I dip again and eat the whole fry. "How old are you?"

"Thirteen." He swirls his fry in the mixture and comes up with more goop than fry. He leans in to take a bite to keep from dripping it on his shirt. "Yum," he says.

"You got some on your chin."

He wipes it. "What happened to your buddy?"

"Sherri?"

"Yeah. I haven't seen her around lately."

"They moved to Oregon."

His brows knit together. "Didn't they just move here?"

My mouth is full. I nod. I'm not going to tell him why they left.

Out of the corner of my eye, I see Amanda carry her tray to the drop-off window.

"What did you mean when you said your mother has given up trying to cure you?"

"After I came out to my parents, my mother did a lot of research online. She thought maybe my *issue*—air quotes— was a testosterone problem. No such luck." He gives a short, dry laugh. "They still make me go to a therapist, but he's cool."

Amanda marches toward us with her chin in the air. When she's opposite our table, she sticks her tongue out at us. Gabe grabs his chest like he's been stabbed. Not since Sherri left nearly a month ago has there been anyone to stand up for me. It feels pretty nice and even nicer because it's Gabe. I wonder how long it will take Amanda to scrape his sparkly name off her notebook.

"Have you started blockers?" Gabe asks.

I am watching Lacey follow Amanda across the courtyard, shoulders hunched like a rabbit. I feel a little sorry that she hooked her star to Amanda. She's pretty nice when Amanda's not around.

"What?"

"Blockers. Have you started on them?"

Even though it's warm in the cafeteria, goose bumps spread up my arms. "No."

"Aren't you worried about getting facial hair and your voice changing?"

"Of course I am." I'm no longer hungry. "How do you know about them?"

"Mom hoped there was some supplement I could take to not be gay anymore."

My stomach churns. "I live with stepparents. I can't talk to them about anything like blockers."

"Once stuff like that starts to happen, it's irreversible."

"I know that!" I push the rest of my lunch away.

CHAPTER 32

I

O n Saturday, I'm down helping Maddy fill the bird
feeders. It's probably because of all that's happened
this week, but I'm missing Mom more than usual.
Maybe that's what makes me ask Maddy if she believes in
reincarnation.

She must see how full of hope my question is because
she shakes her head and says, "I honestly don't know,
sweetie, but Voltaire said, 'It's no more surprising to be
born twice than it is to be born once; everything in nature
is resurrection.'"

"I like that. Who's Voltaire?"

"A seventeenth-century French writer and philosopher."

"I want to believe in it."

"I know, honey. Most of us do."

With the weight of the feeder off the hook, the branch it
hangs from is now out of Maddy's reach. I take it, add another scoop of sunflower seeds, and rehang it for her.

"You're growing, and I'm shrinking." Maddy pats my
back. "I was about to make a sandwich, you want one?"

"Tuna?"

"Sure."

"Could you fix it like Mom used to with sweet relish instead of celery?"

"I could do that."

"Okay, then."

"You know, Finch, reincarnation or not, your mom is part of those two trees of yours. I've been reading an interesting book about the ability of plants to communicate."

"Like talk to each other?"

She nods. "In a way. They send chemical signals—" She still groans a little when she takes the step up into the house.

"Someone coined the term 'wood-wide-web' to explain how they warn each other of insect invasions and share resources. So much of nature is still beyond our comprehension, but if I were you, I'd take comfort in knowing your mother is very much right there." She nods toward my redwoods. "And is part of the very air you breathe and part of a life-form with more awareness than we give them credit for."

‖

Every year Maddy has to renew her fish and game rehab license, and one of the requirements is to attend at least one conference on wildlife rehabilitation. This year she's in Reno for a week, and I'm taking care of the animals.

Before and after school, I cross the yard headed for the trail to Maddy's—where Ben waits for me every morning and every evening, sitting regally with his front paws together. When he sees me, he's on his feet, tail wagging, and runs to meet me. Each time my heart feels split wide open.

This morning I get out a couple of mice and a frozen chick and leave them to defrost on top of the freezer. I put Ben's food out and feed the cats. I'm coming back down from feeding Otus and Rav, when Ben, who was sitting about four feet from his bowl, leaps into the air like a cat after a butterfly.

A few feet away are two ravens. They take turns robbing Ben's bowl. One stands guard while the other struts over and steals a bite of kibble. Ben yawns, scratches his ear, but when the raven gets close enough to snatch a bite, he jumps at it and barks. They fly a few feet away, then land and swagger toward his bowl again.

I can tell the ravens know this is a game. Ben isn't guarding his dish. He's giving them plenty of room and time to walk over before leaping at them again. When I laugh, he looks at me, jumps up for real, barks at them, and runs toward me. The ravens finish off his breakfast.

Ben and I walk to the creek. He's picked up a stick, which he drops in front of me. I throw it; he retrieves it and brings it back for me to toss again. We do this all the way to my nest between the redwoods. We're right where I put Mom's ashes when his ears go up and he whines. When he looks up like he hears or sees something, my heart lurches. Can he sense what I can no longer see or hear?

CHAPTER 33

T his morning Ben's not waiting for me. I call for him over and over as I walk to Maddy's. After I feed everyone else, and he still hasn't shown up, I really begin to worry. With my heart in my throat, I climb the driveway and look both ways, terrified that he's been hit by a car. If he was, his body isn't anywhere I can see it.

"Ben?" I walk the edge of the pavement, up one side and down the other, scanning the shoulder and the steep drop-off to the ditch.

Back at home, I hear Stan's chainsaw. I take that trail, in case Ben's with him, though he treats Stan the way he used to treat me, running from him, tail tucked.

"Have you seen Ben?" I ask when I get Stan's attention.

"Nope."

"I can't imagine he went back to *that* place, but I'm going to ride out to see."

"Be careful."

"I will."

I ride slowly, looking right and left, to see if he's been hit somewhere between here and there. All I find at his old place are two abandoned cars, more garbage, and a rusty washing machine. Someone has stolen the four concrete blocks the trailer once stood on, and the steps.

I ride home as fast as I can, calling his name all the way. Once home, I call the Humane Society. The girl who answers says there was a dog dropped off last night, but the sheet doesn't show how big or what color.

I can still hear the chainsaw, so I ride my bike down the trail into the woods. The branch Stan's cutting cracks loose and falls the fifty feet to the ground. "We have to go to the Humane Society!" I shout just as the chainsaw dies.

"Jesus. You scared me."

"I can't find Ben."

"He'll show up when he gets hungry."

"No. Something's happened to him. I'm sure of it."

"Well, what do you want me to do?"

"We need to go to the Humane Society and see if he's there."

"I can't drive you there. I've got another month to go on my suspension. Cindee's with her client out on Pudding Creek today. She'll be home about five."

"They close at five."

"Look, let me finish this tree, then we'll talk about what to do."

"Please hurry."

When the saw starts again, screaming through the next limb, I close my eyes. *Please let Ben be okay.*

The chainsaw stops, and I look up. Stan is rappelling down the trunk.

I hug him when he reaches the ground. "Thank you."

II

Stan decides if we get stopped with me behind the wheel we'll be in less trouble than if he gets pulled over. The speed limit on this section of Highway 20 is 50 miles per hour, but I'm driving 35. Cars accumulate behind us in a long line.

"Take that pull-off." Stan's jumpy with me behind the wheel, which makes me more nervous. "Put your signal on."

The gravel pelts the underside of the truck like BBs. Eight cars pass before I signal and pull back out onto the highway. Another hundred yards, and Stan points to Summers Lane, the turnoff to the Humane Society. I put my left-turn signal on, and slow. A logging truck is coming from the other direction and roars by us, rocking the 4×4.

"I'm not sure I'll ever get used to driving."

"You're doing fine," Stan says. "It's better to be cautious."

Summers Lane is paved for the first half mile or so, then turns to dirt. Rain has filled the potholes. I try to steer around and between them, but there are dozens, and one tire or the other plops in, creating a muddy splash.

"Don't worry about it. You can't hurt this old truck."

The road to the Humane Society is so unmaintained, I'm surprised at how modern and clean the building is. Ben's new blue collar is on the dashboard of the truck. It arrived in the mail last week, but I've been waiting for the sore on his neck to heal. B-E-N and our phone number are stitched on it in gold. I also brought the leash I found among all the cages and feeders at Maddy's. I grab the leash and the collar and jump down from the truck.

Outside, under the overhang, is a carpeted tower as tall as I am. A cat is asleep at the top. I pet it before going in.

"Are you Finch?" the man behind the desk asks.

"Yes, sir. Chuck?"

"Yes."

"Is he here?"

"I don't know. We have sixty dogs at the moment, and most are large dogs. I'll take you back to the kennels."

The barking grows louder as Stan and I follow Chuck along the corridors, and it becomes deafening when he pushes through a door that opens into a concrete room full of chain-link cages. Every cage holds two or three sad-eyed dogs. All of them run to the wire, tails wagging, and bark for attention.

Stan puts a comforting hand on my shoulder. "They all hope you're here for them."

"I know." I kneel in front of the first cage and hook my fingers through the wire. The tongues of three small Chihuahua-sized dogs lick my fingertips, their tails wagging so hard I wonder how their little spines don't snap.

In the cage behind me, three large dogs beg for attention. Farther down, another leaps into the air over and over. If there weren't a top layer of wire, he would easily jump up and out of the cage. Next to it is a young boxer; he bows to me, butt up, his stubby tail whipping side to side. It's when I lean down to touch him through the wire that I see that each cage has an opening to an outside concrete run. If Ben is here, he will be as far away from this commotion as he can get.

I walk along looking in every cage. When I come to an empty one, I squat down, trying to see through the plastic-flap-covered opening to the run. "Ben," I call at each one, which spurs the dogs to start barking again.

I make a complete loop back to where Stan and Chuck are waiting. "He's not in any of the cages, but I can't see outside."

"We'll go out there, then." Chuck leads us out a side door. All the dogs with access to the outside burst through the plastic flaps and follow us.

I walk the line of pens, look back at Stan, and shake my head.

Chuck pats my shoulder. "If the sheriff picked him up, he'll be taken to Animal Control in Ukiah, but if they just got him this morning, they may not have taken him over yet. Why don't you try their office?"

I drive us back to town and park a block from the sheriff's station so no one will see me behind the wheel.

"I can't go in with you," Stan says. "If they see me, they may want to know how I got here."

"It's okay," I say, but my stomach feels as full of earthworms as Maddy's compost bin.

After I explain the situation to the officer at the desk, he makes a phone call. I pick the cuticles of the two nails I broke untying the rope around Ben's neck until the officer hangs up the phone, and shakes his head sadly. "He left an hour ago with the dogs."

"Was one of them a big beige dog, part ridgeback? He has a scar on the top of his head that looks like someone shot at him, and a sore on his neck."

"Yep. He bit the guy who caught him."

"He's afraid of everybody but me."

"You're telling me. We've been trying to catch that dog for months."

"Why?" My voice shakes.

"We had numerous calls that he was a road hazard."

"He used to live out at the end of our road, but he lives with us now."

The officer looks at his computer screen. "You live at 15210 McDowell Creek?"

I nod.

"Yep. That's where we got him. He'd been seen sitting at that school bus stop, so we set the trap there."

A physical pain starts in my chest and spreads. "He was waiting for me."

"I'm really sorry—" He looks at my address on his computer screen, then at me. I can see him trying to decide if I'm a boy or a girl. "—Miss Delgado. If he'd had a collar on . . ."

"I have one." I hold it up for him to see. "I was waiting for the sore on his neck to heal."

"That's always the way. Just when a problem is about to be solved, it gets worse. I'm afraid you'll have to go to Ukiah to get him."

Back in the truck, I put my head against the steering wheel. Stan strokes my head the same way I stroke Ben's.

CHAPTER 34

"You've got my dog." I'm on the phone with Animal Control in Ukiah.

There's silence on the other end, then the woman's voice says, "And a lot of other people's."

"He's big and yellow, and his name is Ben."

"Is that the name on his collar?" Her voice is reproachful, like she knows the answer.

"He wasn't wearing a collar, but I have one for him now."

"That's good."

"The sheriff here in Fort Bragg remembers him and told me they took him over to you. What do I have to do to get him back?"

"First you need to come over and identify him. We have about seventy dogs here. Quite a few are big, yellow, and probably named Ben."

"The hair is missing in a circle around his neck caused by a rope."

"Really?"

"Not from me. The people who abandoned him tied him to a tree and drove away."

"So he's not *your* dog?"

"He is now. I rescued him."

"You still have to come here to retrieve him—*and* if he hasn't been neutered, we will do that, give him his shots, test for heartworms, and implant a microchip. You'll have to pay for those services."

"Do you have to do all that?"

"It's required before we can release him back to his owner."

"How much is all that?"

"About one hundred and fifty dollars depending on the number of vaccinations he needs, and whether we have to neuter him or not."

These people stole my dog. *What a rip-off,* I think, but don't say it out loud.

Maddy paid me ten dollars a day for taking care of the animals while she was in the hospital and Sherwood Oaks so I have the money, and I won't be using it to go see my father ever again.

"Are you still there?" the woman says.

"Yes, ma'am. If I promise to have all those things done, can't you just bring him back? We're his new family."

"First of all, I don't know which dog is yours, but even if I did, we have policies and procedures. You'll have to come here."

My mind races: Maddy's out of town; Stan can't drive; I can't drive all the way to Ukiah. It's an hour and a half over twisty mountain roads. Cindee's missed a lot of work when she was sick and can't get off again. "I might be able to get my stepmom to drive me over on Monday."

"We're not open on Mondays."

"How long do you keep them before you kill them?"

"Usually four days, longer if the owner calls."

I release the breath I was holding in relief. "Okay, I'll be over as soon as I can find a ride."

"Does your dog happen to have a scar on the top of his head?"

"Yes. That's him. He must be scared out of his wits. He only likes me and my friend Maddy."

There's the sound of someone typing at the other end.

"Hello," I say after a long silence.

"I'm sorry to tell you this," the woman says, "but that dog bit the officer who trapped him."

"I know. Getting trapped scared him."

"Our policy is very clear about animals that bite. He'll be quarantined for the next two days, after which he *will* be put down."

"No!" Tears pool. "He's mine. Please, you can't kill my dog."

"No exceptions."

"He only bit because he was afraid."

"I'm sorry. The policy is quite clear." Her voice is stony.

"Please. He's a wonderful dog." I start to cry. "Please, please."

"Sorry." I think I hear a click like she's hung up.

"Hello?"

||

can go on Monday," Cindee says.

"They're not open Mondays."

"I have to work the rest of the week." She turns back to *Entertainment Tonight*, which she tapes and watches every morning.

"What am I going to do?" I say more to myself than to Cindee.

"You said there were dozens of dogs at the pound. We'll get you another one."

I stare at Cindee's back. She's at the counter, a slice of toast poised in front of her open mouth, but she's so totally engrossed in what the future holds for the latest contestant voted off *American Idol* she's forgotten to take a bite.

The remote is next to the toaster. I pick it up and turn the TV off.

"Darn it. The power's gone off again." Cindee looks around and sees the remote in my hand. "I was watching that."

"I don't want another dog. I love Ben, and he loves me."

Cindee puts the toast down. "I'm sorry. You're right. What do you want me to do?"

"She knew I was just a kid. Maybe if you call—"

Cindee nods. I punch in the number and hand her the phone. As soon as Cindee identifies herself and why she's calling, I overhear the same woman saying exactly what she said when I called as if she was reading from a script.

The color begins to rise in Cindee's cheeks. "What kind of sense does that make? He bit because he was traumatized. I'd have bitten the guy, too."

The woman says something I miss, but Cindee grips the side of the counter. "Why, in God's name, would you insist on killing an animal that has a loving home waiting for him?"

"Rules are rules," is the muffled response.

"You have not heard the end of this. We know people." She slams the phone down so hard the battery cover pops off. "What bull. It's bureaucrats like her—on their tiny little power trips—who are responsible for most of what's wrong with the world."

I'm not listening. *Now what?* I pick up the phone, replace the battery cover, and put it back on the charger. "Do *you* know anyone who can help?"

Cindee shakes her head. "Not really, but surely Maddy does. Have you called her?"

"I can't find where I put her cell number, and I don't remember which hotel she's in."

"Where did you look?"

"Everywhere."

"Look, Finch, I think I made things worse—if that's possible."

I agree, but I say, "No, you didn't."

"Why don't you call her back, apologize, and tell her Ben's story. Maybe somewhere beneath that rock-hard shell, a heart still beats."

"It can't get much worse, can it?"

Cindee smiles wryly. "We could let Stan try."

I actually laugh, because it's true. Stan, when he's mad, can be scary, but I also would never have guessed that Cindee could have a moment of clarity when it comes to *her man*.

I hold the phone for a long time, finally take a deep breath, and push Redial. It rings five times before a recording about their hours of operation starts. I'm about to hang up when the woman answers, and says hello.

"I'm calling to apologize." I glance at Cindee. The recorded message plays over her voice. When it ends, I repeat my apology. "My stepmother was trying to help."

"Apology accepted. I'm only following procedures."

"I understand. It's just . . ." My voice cracks. "My mother

is dead and before she died, my father left us because he didn't want to stay married to a woman with . . . cancer. Ben's family—the people he loved—tied him to a tree and drove away. He was on the road every day because he hoped they'd come back for him, but he had to eat. He came every day, twice a day, to my friend Maddy's house to be fed, then walked the mile back home to wait. He even collected all the things they left behind, including a broken doll and charred beer cans, and put them in a pile, and slept near them."

I've been talking with my back to Cindee so she couldn't watch me tell Ben's story. I turn now. Tears streak Cindee's face. I close my eyes. "I had a pile of keepsakes, too. Things I found and kept of my father's because I thought he'd want me back someday. But when I found him, he didn't want me. He'd moved on, just like Ben's family. That sheriff's deputy trapped Ben at my school bus stop. Don't you see? Ben loves me now. He won't be on the road anymore, and he doesn't deserve to die."

Cindee blows her nose.

At the other end is only silence.

"Are you there?" I say.

"Yes." Her voice is barely a whisper.

I wait.

"I went to look at your dog after your stepmother called. I remember him. He was adopted as a puppy from the shelter in Fort Bragg. I used to work next door at the animal control facility there. He was the sole survivor of a litter of puppies shot by their owner. That scar on his head is a graze from a bullet wound."

There's another long moment during which I say nothing. Either this woman's heart will open, or her mind will close again. I look at Cindee, who is on a stool on the far side of the counter, her head bowed over prayer hands, the first two fingers of which are crossed for luck.

"There's one exception to the rule," the woman says.

My heart skips.

At the muffled sound of the woman speaking, Cindee opens her eyes.

"If you can find a nonprofit animal rescue facility that will take him, we can turn him over to them."

I squeeze my lips together to keep from whooping.

Cindee looks skyward. "Thank you, Jesus," she whispers.

"I can give you some names," the woman says.

"Thank you so much," I say, "but our next—"

Cindee shakes her head and puts a finger to her lips.

"I'd love a list." I grab a pencil to write *Bones* in Covelo and *Second Chance Rescue* in Fort Bragg at the bottom of Cindee's shopping list.

"I hope one or the other will help you," the woman says. "You have two days left."

"Yes, ma'am. I know. Thank you." Then I remember the money. "Will I still need the hundred and fifty dollars?"

"No. We aren't giving him to you, and we don't charge nonprofits."

"Okay."

"One other thing." Her voice has that I'm-in-charge edge again. "He'll still have to pass all the behavioral analysis tests."

"He will." I'm afraid to ask what that entails.

"Maybe," she says.

"Why didn't you want me to tell her about Maddy?" I ask after I hang up.

"That woman wants to be kowtowed to. She needs to be the hero here. If you tell her how easy it will be to fulfill that requirement, she may throw another obstacle in your way."

I've learned a few valuable lessons in the last couple of weeks: understand your enemy, evaluate who is worthy of trust, and cut your stepmom a lot of slack. Cindee's turning out to be much wiser than I would ever have imagined.

"When is Maddy due back?"

"Monday or Tuesday."

"Did I hear her say you have until Thursday?"

I nod. "But I still want to call Maddy. She needs to know what's happening."

"I agree. Why not call her house?"

"What good would that do? She's not there."

Cindee smiles. "Maybe she left her contact information on her answering machine."

"Of course she did." I run around the counter and give Cindee a quick hug.

Her smile this time is sad. "I'm not always as dumb as I look."

"You don't look dumb." I sound lame.

"Yes, I do. I bleach my hair, talk like a Valley girl, and start every sentence with 'This is probably stupid,' or 'This probably won't work but—'" Her lips compress. "My only real talent is I can wiggle my ears."

"Can you?"

She smiles once more, then faces me and begins to tighten and loosen the muscles in her face. Her ears wiggle like a rabbit's nose.

I giggle and try it, but only manage to lift and lower my eyebrows.

"You have other talents," Cindee says. "You are tall and beautiful and smart as a whip—" Before I can deny all those things, Cindee adds, "I've been meaning to ask you where you got those earrings."

She means the small diamond ear studs. I've started wearing them now that Stan is off my case about being trans. "Mom gave these to me on my tenth birthday."

Cindee looks confused. "But she passed—"

"I know. Four months before my birthday. She gave them to Maddy to give me, just in case."

"I'm glad, Finch. She's with our Lor— Sorry, I know you hate when I say things like that."

"It's okay. What you believe doesn't have to be what I believe. For me she's part of the trees and the creek and the air I breathe. That's what works for me." I lean and kiss Cindee's pink, powdered cheek. "Mom's glad you're here keeping an eye on me."

"I have to be honest. I've never loved anyone the way I love Stan. I guess you know that. And he only married me to get help raising you."

"Yeah, but he loves you now."

"That's nice of you to say."

"It's true. He told me so."

"He did?" She puts a hand to her heart.

"When you were sick, I found him in the shed praying you'd be okay."

Tears spill down her cheeks again. She takes a napkin from the holder next to the police scanner. "He was praying?"

"Looked like it. Said he was afraid he'd lose you, too."

"Oh, Finch, thank you." She takes both my hands in hers. "Thank you . . ." Her voice catches. ". . . for telling me." She puts her arms around me and cries softly against my shoulder.

I stroke her brittle blond hair. My eyes are drawn to the lace curtains over the sink, and I realize that all along, Cindee has been trying her best to make a home for us out of someone else's house.

"There, there," I say, like Mom used to say to me.

CHAPTER 35

I

If this weren't Ben's life we were talking about, Maddy's reaction to the news would have been funny. I've never heard her use language like that. It takes her a few minutes to gain control. Sorry, she says, only to launch again into what idiots they are. Her breathing becomes ragged.

"Okay." She pauses. "I have two more sessions to attend today, but I can leave Reno in the morning and meet you in Ukiah."

"How long will it take you to get there?"

"Six hours. I'll leave at eight and be there by two or so. Can Cindee bring you over?"

"She has to work, but I'll think of something."

"Finch, before they release him to me—if they release him to me—they're going to put him through some tests."

"What will they want him to do?"

"Not show aggression, for one, especially food aggression. Whether they can put a leash on him, and if he'll let them check his teeth. Do you think he'll make it through them?"

"I don't know, Maddy. I can't imagine that they can get him to do anything, but I know he would do it for me."

"Well, try not to worry," she says, but she sounds worried.

II

Gabe and I have started meeting every day for lunch. He keeps glancing at me while we eat. "Why are you so quiet?"

"Animal Control has my dog."

"I didn't know you had a dog."

"He's a stray my neighbor was feeding, but he's mine now."

"Why do they have him?"

I tell him the whole story about Ben. I tell him I don't know how I'm going to get to Ukiah since Stan can't drive and Cindee is working.

Gabe helps himself to one of my French fries. "Why not take the bus?"

"There's a bus?"

"There are two. One at seven thirty in the morning and another at ten thirty. I used to have asthma. Mom and I took it to Ukiah once a week for my shots. What time is your neighbor going to meet you?"

"Two o'clock, but I'd rather take the early one. Maybe they'd let me sit with Ben until Maddy gets there."

It's a nice day, and we're at one of the picnic tables. I spot Amanda and Lacey coming out of the cafeteria. Amanda is walking like a duck with her back arched, stomach sticking out, mimicking the way Rita Casey, who is crossing the courtyard, has to walk because she's so heavy. Rita has dyed her hair again. Today it's green.

Gabe turns to look where I'm looking. "Why does she do that?"

"Because she's mean."

"I know why Amanda does it. Why does Rita give haters more ammunition?"

I shrug. "Maybe 'cause she's going to be bullied anyway and she'd rather it be for her hair color than her size."

Gabe blinks. "That's probably it, isn't it?" He covers my hand with his. Before I can take it away, Amanda spots us and his hand on mine. Her eyes narrow and her lips curl in a sneer.

Lacey glances at Amanda.

"Lookee there, the fairy and the freak are in love."

My breath catches. How does Amanda know Gabe's gay? An accidental guess? What if he thinks I told someone? I didn't. I glance at him.

Gabe swings his legs out from under the table and stands up. "How perceptive of you, Amanda. I was just about ask Finch to the dance Saturday. Are you and your shadow going?"

"I hate you."

"That's a real shame. We're both crazy about you, aren't we, Finch?"

"That's a stupid name," Amanda says.

"I like it," Gabe says. "You'll have to tell me how you got it when we're at the dance."

Amanda marches off, with Lacey trailing her.

"How do you manage to think on your feet like that?"

"Practice." Gabe gathers our empty plates. "I mean it about the dance. Want to go?"

I feel myself blush. "I don't know how to dance."

"I'll teach you."

"I don't have anything to wear."

"Well, while we're in Ukiah waiting for your neighbor, we'll go shopping." He dumps our paper plates in the trash.

"You want to go to Ukiah with me?"

"Why not? I'm great moral support."

CHAPTER 36

I

Tuesday dawns cold and foggy. Cindee and I wait in the car with the heater running until Gabe shows up. While we wait, I tell her about Gabe inviting me to the dance.

"What will you wear?"

I shrug. I long ago outgrew my church dress and the one Maddy bought me for Mom's funeral.

Cindee opens her bag, takes out her wallet, and hands me a twenty, then another. "There's a Walmart at the south end of town. Get something pretty."

"I'll pay you back."

She shakes her head. "I'd like whatever you find to be my gift."

II

Fort Bragg is on the Pacific Ocean, and divided from inland Mendocino County by the Coast Ranges, two side-by-side chains of low mountains. To get to Ukiah, the bus turns east on Highway 20, a twisty two-lane road. This morning's fog still lies in the valleys, which makes the tops of the mountains look like tree-covered islands floating on a fluffy white sea.

Gabe's oddly quiet. I start worrying he thinks I told someone who then told Amanda he's gay.

"I didn't tell anybody."

He looks confused. "Didn't tell anybody what?"

We're sitting in the next-to-the-last row. I glance behind me. "That you're gay," I whisper.

"I didn't think you did."

"It was weird that Amanda called you a . . . you know."

"She was trying to insult me. To her we were two boys holding hands. She didn't know she'd nailed it."

Gabe goes quiet again and closes his eyes. By the time we get to the worst part of Highway 20, where it becomes all sharp turns and switchbacks, he's a pale shade of green.

"Change seats with me," Gabe says after the first sharp turn. He doesn't look too good.

I climb over his knees and he moves next to the window, lowers it, and leans against the glass with the wind in his face.

"Why didn't you tell me you get carsick?"

"I was hoping I wouldn't this time."

He suffers for another fifteen minutes until we reach the straightaway into Willits and head south to Highway 101.

III

Animal Control is at the very south end of Ukiah. We get off the bus and wait ten minutes at the Pear Tree shopping center for the number 9 local, which drops us off at the end of Plant Road. From there it's a short walk to Animal Control. Nine thirty in the morning and the parking lot is nearly full.

Turns out Tuesday is adoption day. The lobby is swarming with people enjoying the antics of kittens in cages stacked one on top of the other along two of the walls. Off to the right is a Meet & Greet room where people can spend a little time with the dog they are interested in. Pictures of dog adoption successes are strung like flags on a cord that stretches from one end of the room to the other. Along the corridor are "before" pictures of skeletal dogs, some with hideous skin infections, beside "after" pictures of the same dogs, fully recovered and healthy looking.

Gabe and I make our way to the front desk. "May I help you?" says the woman behind it.

"I'd like to visit my dog. He was picked up in Fort Bragg."

"Your name?"

"Finch Delgado. His name is Ben."

The woman looks down a list of dogs, then up at me. "I'm sorry. He's in quarantine and on the list to be euthanized. You can't see him."

"I . . . We came all—"

"Sorry. May I help you?" she says to the person behind us.

"Please."

Gabe puts his arm around my shoulder and turns me away from the desk. "Come with me."

Once we're outside, he says, "They aren't going to let you see him."

"I know."

"How long before your friend gets here?"

"Not until two."

We step away from the front entrance to let the parents of an excited little boy go in. "Shhhh." His mother puts a finger to her lips before opening the door. "You need to use the same voice you use to talk to your sister." His mother cups her baby bump.

"Okay," the little boy whispers.

Watching this mom with her son makes me miss my mother almost more than I can stand. I bite down hard on my lip to keep from crying.

"Finch?" Gabe's voice seems far away. "Finch," he says again.

"I hear you."

"I know you're scared and upset, but your friend will get him released. There's no point in hanging out here if they won't let you see him."

"I know."

"And think how awful it would be for him, if he saw you for a few minutes, and then you left him here." He looks at his watch. "He wouldn't know you'd be back in four hours."

I hadn't thought of what seeing me would mean to Ben. Gabe's right. He wouldn't understand my leaving.

"There was a Ross at that first bus stop," Gabe says. "Let's go find you a dress for the dance and have some lunch. We'll come back at two to meet your friend."

IV

I sit staring out the window on the ride back to the Pear Tree shopping center. Out of the corner of my eye, I can see Gabe watching me. "It'll be okay." His tone is the same as Maddy's when she told me not to worry. I know wishful thinking when I hear it. I'm practically an expert.

"Those people want to kill Ben." I'm swallowing to keep from crying.

Gabe squeezes my hand but says nothing.

Mom got my church dress online, and Maddy ordered my funeral dress the same way. There are no big stores in Fort Bragg, so I've never been in a place like Ross. Gabe and I walk the aisles until we find the Juniors section. I don't even know what size I wear. Gabe picks out a couple he likes. One has a pink top and flowered skirt, the other looks like a red Native American rug with zigzaggy stripes. He holds up first one, then the other in front of me. I shake my head. "I like dull colors."

Gabe smiles. "Let's say you like less showy colors. There's nothing dull about you."

I don't see anything I like and can't seem to focus on seriously looking. Gabe holds up a black one that fits my mood. It's high-waisted, with a pleated skirt and—since I don't have any boobs—spaghetti straps to keep the top from falling down. I take it in all three sizes and drape them over my arm.

At the entrance to the dressing rooms, a girl counts how many dresses I'm carrying and hands me a disk with 3 on it. I start to tell her they are all the same because I don't know what size I wear, but she's way too bored to care.

I walk past all the closed doors to the last dressing room. There's no lock on the door, so I drape my coat over the top to show it's occupied. I strip down and stand in front of the mirror in my boys' underwear. To keep from going crazy with hatred for my body, I never look at myself in the full-length mirror at home. Seeing myself exposed as what I am on the outside—a scrawny boy—makes me ache inside.

The size 7 dress fits best but it's short on me; the 9 looks like I'm wearing a black sack.

"Finch?"

I open the door and stick my head out. Gabe waves from the entrance.

I step out, hold my arms up, and turn a full circle.

"It's too big." He glances at the guard girl. She's filing her nails. "My sister," he says, and walks past her. She looks up, sees he's not carrying anything, and goes back to filing.

"Wait there." I go in and close the door. When I come out again, I'm wearing the size 7. I can see how pretty I look in his eyes. "Wow," he says.

His reaction at least makes me smile.

CHAPTER 37

I

It's one thirty when we get back to Animal Control. There's a white Prius in the parking lot. I look in the window. It's neat and clean. Not Maddy's. Hers is always a mess.

Inside the center is still crowded. Young volunteers lead people from door to door to look at the adult cats. Gabe and I join a group looking in through a window into a room lined with small cages, each holding a cat. Two cats are asleep on a carpeted tower, another plays with one of the toys that litter the floor.

"This is where we socialize the cats so they get used to being around other cats," the volunteer says.

A little boy holds his arms up, and his father lifts him so he can look through the window.

I see myself swim to my father, feel myself being lifted and tossed back into the water. I swim to him again and again to be picked up and tossed. Even back then, he was throwing me away. Goose bumps rise on my arms. Instead of being the memory that led me to search for him, it should have been the one that told me to leave well enough alone.

There are small dogs in cages in the next room. The

closest one to the window holds what looks like a purebred Yorkshire terrier. The cage is roomy, but she's running in a tight square, tail tucked, ears pinned.

"What's the matter with that little dog?" the woman next to me asks.

"She was rescued from a puppy mill, where she spent five years in a wire cage the same size as the square she is making," the volunteer says. "She'd gotten too old to breed any longer so they tried to drown her in a water barrel. She was hanging on to the rim when the Humane Society raided the place."

"How long had she been there?" the woman asks.

"They don't know. She was standing on the bodies of other dogs. She probably will never make a good pet, but no one has the heart to deny her a chance."

"Oh, Jim," the woman says. "Let's take her."

"This dog will need someone with a lot of time on their hands," the volunteer says. "She likes to be held, but the minute you put her down, she paces like that."

"That just breaks my heart," the woman says. "But we both work."

"She'll be all right. There's a woman coming from Second Chance Rescue in Fort Bragg. They will rehabilitate her and find her a good home."

Across the hall from the adoptable dogs are four doors marked "Quarantine Area: Authorized Personnel Only." I look through each of the rectangular windows but can only see into the first cage in each row.

We've reached the end of the hallway. The girl opens a door to the outside kennels. It's a roofed open area with dozens of cages. The relentless barking is deafening. Gabe holds the door for the young couple with the little boy.

"What are the clothespins for?" I ask. Attached to many of the cages are signs saying "You Can Take Me Home Today," held in place by different-colored clothespins.

"We have a color for each day. Volunteers take the dogs for walks and this lets us know who's been walked and who hasn't." The girl practically has to shout to be heard. "There are two play areas here, so all the dogs get a chance to run around a bit."

I look down the side of the building. There is a ten-foot space between it and a tall board fence. There's one deflated ball. Opposite the cages of barking dogs is another wide play area with a few more toys.

Nearly every cage holds a pit bull, or pit bull mix. Only one has a couple of small dogs, but they cower when the little boy squats down to look at them.

"We don't want a pit bull," his mother says.

"All of these are fine family dogs, but people are afraid to take a chance," the volunteer says.

"I'm just as afraid," she says. "Sorry."

I glance over my shoulder. Maddy's face is in the window.

I wave, grab Gabe's hand, and tug him toward the door, but my heart begins to pound. Maddy's grim expression frightens me.

"What's the matter?" I close the door against the chaotic, hopeful barking.

Maddy and Gabe nod to each other.

I remember my manners. "Maddy, this is Gabe."

They shake hands.

"Something's wrong." My voice cracks.

Maddy shakes a crumpled form in her fist. "These idiots," she hisses under her breath, "won't let me claim him. My license is for wildlife rehabilitation. Only a licensed pet rescue organization or a companion animal group can claim him."

My stomach churns. "What are we going to do? His quarantine is up the day after tomorrow."

"I got them to agree to give us more time, but they've got over sixty dogs. I don't want to leave him here and hope they comply, or even remember."

"My father's an attorney," Gabe says. "I'll call him and see if there's something he can do." He has a hand on my shoulder.

Maddy sighs. "I'm willing to try anything, but I'm afraid they are so rigid in this place, they will parrot the same policy to him. If I hear 'rules are rules' from that Bliss woman one more time, *I'm* going bite someone."

"Her name is Bliss?" I say.

"Isn't that a corker?"

II

Maddy, Gabe, and I sit in the lobby waiting to hear back from a woman Maddy knows at Bones Pet Rescue in Covelo, and another at the Milo Foundation near Willits. I watch the hand on the wall clock skip from minute to minute. It reminds me again of sitting in Mom's hospital room watching it steal her remaining time. Now it's stealing Ben's.

Gabe tries to call his dad again. An hour goes by.

A black kitten in the cage opposite where we sit is chasing its own tail. A little girl runs over to watch, but the kitten scampers to join its sibling in the corner and stares at her with frightened blue eyes.

Every time a car pulls into the parking lot, sunlight flashes off its windshield, and we all turn to look. This time, it's a gray van. When the driver steps out, Maddy claps her hands together and grins. "Well, Lord love a duck. There is a god."

"What?"

"That's my friend Jeanne, from Second Chance Rescue in Fort Bragg."

"She's here to pick up that Yorkshire terrier," I say to Gabe, and turn to Maddy. "Do you think—?"

"I certainly do." Maddy waves to the woman, who waves back. "Wait here." She gets up and goes out to meet her. They stand and talk for a few minutes. The woman listens and shakes her head sympathetically, lips compressed. Maddy keeps talking, and the woman shakes her head again and turns palms up. Maddy nods toward me. I sit up straighter.

The head shaking turns to a shrug and a nod. Maddy and the woman hug, and Maddy holds the door open for her.

"Finch, I'd like you to meet Jeanne Gocker. And this is Finch's friend Gabe."

Jeanne takes my hand. "Maddy's told me a pretty sad story about this dog of yours."

"Yes, ma'am."

"I've taken other biters, but I can't take responsibility for a vicious dog, so before I do that, we've agreed"—she looks at Maddy— "that if the dog—"

"Ben," I say. "His name is Ben."

"If Ben passes the behavioral tests, I'll accept responsibility for him, sign the necessary papers, and let you adopt him from me."

"Who will give him the test?"

"One of their staff people."

"He'll do anything for me, but I'm not sure he will for anyone else."

Jeanne sighs. "Let's see what happens. I hope you understand. They won't let me sign out a vicious dog."

"He's not vicious." I touch her arm. "He's not. I promise. Please help him." Tears spill down my face. I swipe at them with the heels of my hands.

Maddy puts an arm around my shoulders. "Shhh. It's too early for tears." She hugs me. "Don't worry. We'll get him back if we have to break him out.

Ten minutes later, Bliss, the director, and a man wearing huge padded gloves that reach his elbows come through the door from outside. He's carrying Ben's new blue collar, a leash, and a stick with a rubber glove on the end. Barking echoes along the corridor even after he closes the door.

"Not a man!" I turn to Maddy. "It can't be a man. Everything bad that's ever happened to him was done by a man. He's been shot, beaten, deserted, and trapped by men. They have to give him a chance to pass."

"He's a big dog," Bliss says. "We don't want to send a woman in with him."

"Send me," I say.

"Sorry. No way."

"She's right," Maddy says. "I'll go."

"We can't permit that."

Gabe's phone rings.

He looks at the number. "It's Dad. He turns his back and walks toward the back door. "That's great, Dad. Thanks."

"His father is my attorney," Maddy tells Bliss.

She doesn't look intimidated.

"Dad said if he was trapped on private property, you have a case."

"The school bus stop *is* on our property. Stan built the shed we wait in. They trapped Ben in the shed that belongs to us."

"Sorry." Bliss turns to walk away.

The man unlocks the door to the quarantine section, pats my shoulder, and steps inside. I watch through the small window. The dog in the first cage—a Rottweiler—charges the chain link, snarling and barking. The man walks to the last cage and kneels down.

I close my eyes and press my forehead to the glass. *Ben, please pass.*

The man opens the cage and steps inside. That's all I can see. Minutes pass like stones.

Ms. Gocker comes out of the dog room carrying the Yorkshire terrier. "How's it going?"

"We don't know." Maddy glances at Bliss sitting in her office. "How in the name of God did that woman get her job?"

"I don't know," Ms. Gocker says softly. "Rules first, the animal's welfare last."

I hear the Rottweiler snarling and crashing against his chain-link door. I jump up and run to the window. The man has Ben on the leash.

"Oh wow. He passed!" I throw open the door. "Ben! You passed."

Ben's tail wags so hard his entire back half jerks from side to side. I drop to my knees and the man lets go of my dog. Ben nearly bowls me over, licking my face.

I look up at the man. "He passed."

He glances toward Bliss's office. "Kind of," he whispers. "He has no food aggression, and I was able to put the leash on him after he smelled you on that collar. I didn't try to inspect his teeth. I think he was holding it together because he knew you were out here."

"Thank you."

"You're very welcome. I wish all the dogs that leave here were guaranteed this much love."

CHAPTER 38

"hank your dad for me," Maddy says. We're in the Prius headed back across the mountains. Ben is in the backseat with me with his head in my lap.

Gabe's riding shotgun with the window cracked. He looks back at me. "He never called. That was Verizon with a deal for extra minutes. I made up the private property thing."

Maddy and I laugh. "You're kidding," I say.

Gabe shakes his head.

"How'd you think of it?"

He shrugs. "My dad says there is no reasoning with a petty bureaucrat on a power trip. It seemed worth a try."

My heart aches for Gabe. "I'm sorry he didn't call."

"Thanks. Maybe one of these days—" He turns to look out the window.

"Maddy says a parent's love should be unconditional, like a dog's. Isn't that right, Maddy?"

Her eyes smile at me in the rearview mirror. "In a better world."

II

We stand on Maddy's front deck and watch Ben trot around the yard, sniffing and lifting his leg on every bush and shrub. Two ravens sit in a Doug fir. One swoops down to land on the ground and struts over to the dish of food Maddy put out. Ben barks, races toward it, and leaps into the air when it flies off. I laugh. "I'm so glad he's free to come and go as he pleases."

Maddy laughs. "Dogs do live in the moment, but he's not free."

"What do you mean?"

"Ben doesn't want to roam. All he wants is safety and love and food when he's hungry."

I'm at Maddy's sink making tuna fish the way my mother used to, with relish rather than celery. Gabe is standing in front of the woodstove with his hands held to the heat. "Are all these paintings your work?"

"Most of them." Maddy takes glasses down from the cupboard and gets orange juice from the fridge.

"I like them," Gabe says.

Ben sits on the deck, front paws together, watching us through the window.

"I like that there's a path into all of them," I say.

"I had an art teacher once who said a landscape should have a way in, a way out, a place to hide, and a place to rest." Maddy fills our two glasses and lays the empty juice carton on the floor. I step on it for her and put it in the recycle bag. "These pieces remind me of places I've been and loved—the azaleas in Florida under the sprawling, Spanish moss—covered oaks. Vermont trails through white birches, and hikes here through the redwoods. The paths are there to give you a way in." She pours herself a glass of red wine and comes to sit with us at her kitchen table. "Have you ever noticed how a portrait's eyes follow you wherever you walk in a room?"

"Yeah." I hand Gabe his glass of juice and sit down. "It's creepy."

"It works the same with paintings of paths and roads. Try it with the painting above the woodstove. Walk from one side of the room to the other."

I do, and no matter where I stand, the beginning of the path appears to be directly in front of me. I could move into the picture from any point in the room. "That is so cool.

"Why did you paint this one?" I point to the one of my trail to the waterfall.

Maddy smiles. "For the day you'd ask."

"What do you mean?"

"I painted it for you."

"Really?"

Maddy walks over, lifts the painting off the wall, and hands it to me.

I hug her. "I looked at this every day while you were hurt. Each time I did, the mist from the waterfall seemed to change shape. It made me think of Mom."

"I thought so, too, Finch. I watched you there one day. It looked as if the mist was reaching to touch you. Turn the painting over."

An envelope is taped to the back of the frame. In it is a picture of me and Mom. I remember the day Maddy took it. Mom's hair had grown back full and curly. I'm holding the baby raccoon that Maddy was raising, and it has one of its paws in my mouth trying to steal what I was eating.

"Thank you, Maddy. The only picture I have of Mom is in her prom dress."

Maddy put her arm around my shoulder. "Now you'll always have one of the two of you together."

With Maddy watching from her deck, Ben, Gabe, and I take the trail down to the creek. Ben wades into the water, grabs a stick, and shakes it from side to side.

Over the sound of the waterfall, a tiny brown Pacific wren breaks into song, filling the canyon with music.

CHAPTER 39

1

en follows us to my house, but he still won't come inside. We've moved his bed to our front porch. He curls up in it and puts his head on his paws. No matter how long I'm inside, I know he'll be there when I come out again.

Cindee and Stan are in the kitchen, hugging. Cindee pulls away and blushes. "What's that?" Cindee means the painting under Gabe's arm.

"Maddy gave it to me. This picture of Mom and me was on the back." I hand it to Stan, who looks at it almost too long.

"Let me see," Cindee says.

She studies the photograph. "Your mother was so beautiful, and you look just like her." She smiles up at Stan. His eyes soften and he kisses the top of her head.

I feel bad and wonder if, subconsciously, I'm still trying to hurt Stan for marrying Cindee. Not for the last time, I'm sure, I recall what Maddy told me about the day Mom died. It had been a couple weeks. Maddy and I were sitting on her back deck looking down at where we put Mom's ashes. I told her how mad I was at Stan because he sent me to the kitchen and I wasn't in the room when Mom died. I told her I never planned to forgive him.

"You're wrong about that, Finch," Maddy said. "Your mom was ready to go, but she didn't want you to see her die. And Stan didn't send you to the kitchen. He went with you because that's what your mom wanted. He made the choice to take you out of the room and not be there himself when she passed. He wanted to stay, it broke his heart not to be with her in the end, but they didn't want you to remember her last breath. I was there. Your mom took his hand and told him she wanted ice cream. That poor man stood there, tears streaming down his face, and nodded, then asked you to help him carry the bowls back from the kitchen. After you left, your mom smiled at me and said, 'I'm so very tired, Maddy.' Then she closed her eyes."

II

On Saturday I'm in the hall bathroom getting dressed for the dance. Maddy let the hem out enough so it won't look like I'm wearing a tutu. I'm about to try the dress on when Cindee knocks on the door. "There's a package for you from Maddy."

I wrap a towel around me, open the door, and stick my hand out. The package is from an online shop called Justice. There's a card on top.

"For the Belle of the Ball. Knock 'em dead, sweetheart. Love, Maddy."

Inside is a slightly padded training bra—"convertible"— that can be worn with or without the straps. I put it on and stand on my tiptoes to see how it looks in the medicine cabinet mirror. It's a perfect fit. I pull my new dress over my head, and quietly open the bathroom door. Stan and Cindee are in the kitchen. I sneak down the hall to their room to look at myself in the full-length mirror. In the mirror, in a dress, with my hair at least covering my ears, the girl I am stares back.

Stan and Cindee are kissing. Cindee sees me first and breaks away. "Oh, Finch, you're—" She steps out from under Stan's arm. "You're beautiful." She turns to him. "Isn't she?"

He shakes his head.

"Stan! You promised." She smiles at me and claps her hands together. "We've got great news."

My mind leaps to the most obvious conclusion. *She's pregnant.* "What?"

Cindee grins. "Stan got a job."

"You're kidding."

"No. After he taught himself to limb trees, he applied to a company that trims trees for the power company. He starts next Monday."

"I'm glad." I cross the kitchen and put my arms around my stepfather. He pats my back.

|||

Cindee drives me to the dance. Gabe's mother said she'd bring me home. In the car on the way, I get up the nerve to ask Cindee for permission to start androgen blockers. I looked them up online. They will delay puberty and are completely reversible.

Without looking at me, she says, "It's not my decision."

"Stan's going to say no."

"I don't think he will, but if he does, then it will be for Maddy to decide."

"You know?"

She nods. "Your mom was as smart as she was beautiful. She left nothing to chance."

'm nervous." Gabe and I walk toward the gym.

"How come?"

I shrug. "I can't dance, and Amanda will—"

Gabe stops. "Haven't you figured her out yet?"

"I guess not."

The music coming from the gym is loud. Clumps of girls pass us, giggling and laughing. One glances at Gabe and smiles.

"She's jealous."

I stop. "Of what? Is she dying to be trans?"

"Probably not that, but . . ."

"But what? If she's here, she's gonna see me in a dress—" I look down. "—with boobs. It will make her night."

"What do you care?" He grins. "You're here with her boyfriend."

IV

t's Sunday. Cindee dragged Stan to church to thank God for his new job. Ben and I head to Maddy's.

I chickened out of asking Stan about blockers.

"I've been waiting for this moment," Maddy says when I tell her I want to start androgen blockers.

"Will you tell Stan it's time?"

"I don't need to."

"Maddy, please. I have to start them before puberty. If my voice starts to change—"

She takes up a hand. "I didn't mean it that way, Finch. Stan and I have already talked."

"I don't care what he said." I pull my hand free and start to pace her kitchen. "You have to help me."

"Finch. Relax." She catches my arm and pulls me close. "He said yes. I've already called for an appointment. We'll see the doctor on Monday. Is that soon enough?"

"Really?" I hug her.

"Really."

"How'd you talk him into it?"

"I didn't have to. Cindee did. I don't know what happened with her, but she managed to get him to understand what it's like for you."

Over Maddy's shoulder I see Ben come to sit at the window. When I look at him, his tail wags.

"I'm going to be okay, aren't I, Maddy?"

"Yes, honey. You are."

AUTHOR'S NOTE

Some years ago, I was sitting at my desk and saw a large yellow dog pass, headed up the road, trotting as if he had a place to be. At about the same time, I heard a story on the news about a dog whose family had been in a serious car accident. He'd been in the car with them but had run off into the woods. Several weeks later, a woman on her way to work noticed that the family's belongings, strewn about after the accident and left behind when the vehicle was towed, now sat in a neat pile. Then she spotted their dog sleeping nearby. The dog had gathered his family's belongings and was waiting for them to come back for him. This incident led to the first iteration of *Freeing Finch*.

But the heart of this story was born from my friendship with Dr. Kathryn Rohr and her wife, Linda. In 2015, I got involved with local issues concerning our rural hospital, and met Dr. Bill Rohr, a highly respected orthopedic surgeon, who was about to retire. A few months later, a friend casually mentioned that Bill had undergone gender-affirmation surgery at age seventy, a journey that was covered in the *Washington Post*. Dr. Bill Rohr was now Dr. Kathryn Rohr.

I wrote to Kathryn to express my support, and she was generous enough to share her experience of gender identity with me. I was inspired to participate in programs on gender diversity where I met and talked to transgender children and their families. Several transgender readers have been kind enough to read *Freeing Finch* and offer their opinions and critiques, including Dr. Rohr. Here is what she had to say:

I don't pretend to be a literary critic but recognize when a book is fantastic. The handling of the trans issue as just another challenge in life that's no more or less significant than all the others, is superb. Love, loved it.

ACKNOWLEDGMENTS

I've been involved in one way or another with the Mendocino Coast Writers' Conference for over twenty years. I believe, if it takes a village to raise a child, it takes a community of writers to birth a book. My community of writers call ourselves the Mixed Pickles: Norma Watkins, Katherine Brown, Kate Erickson, Kymberly Bartlo Ainsworth, Lynn Courtney, and Ginny Reed. Others to whom I am indebted include Teresa Sholars, Linda Rohr, Kate Rohr, Susan Bono, Matthew Miksak, Jessica Kotnour, Shirin Bridges, Bethany Brewer, Lar Krug, Richard Gibb, AJ, Anne Kemp, Jessie Holland, Shirley Schott, and, with heartfelt gratitude, Theo Lorenz. Last but not least, my wonderful editor and friend, Susan Chang, and the rest of the Starscape team.

ADDITIONAL READINGS AND LINKS

There are 1.4 million transgender adults in the US.

There are 150,000 (currently known) transgender teens in the US.

There are an unknown number of trans children, however, there are **6 clinics** in the SF Bay Area alone treating 550 trans children.

It is suggested by experts that therapy for trans kids start as early as three, allowing them to "socially transition," which means dress according to the gender they identify as, and change their names.

There is a high degree of depression and subsequent suicide rate among trans teens who aren't permitted to express their gender identity. However, studies show trans children, permitted to express their gender identity, are no more depressed than the norm.

One parent said about allowing her trans child to socially transition, "I'd rather have a live daughter than a dead son."

Katie Couric's Nat. Geo Special
http://deadline.com/2016/07/katie-couric-next-documentary-looks-at-gender-revolution-for-natgeo-1201795739/

What Does God Think?: Transgender People and The Bible
by Cheryl B. Evans (Author), Colby Martin (Foreword)

Becoming Nicole: The Inspiring Story of Transgender Actor-Activist Nicole Maines and Her Extraordinary Family
by Amy Ellis Nutt

"Causes of Transgender Disorders" on page 78 taken from
http://thefederalist.com/2015/01/09/heres-what-parents
-of-transgender-kids-need-to-know/

https://depts.washington.edu/transyp/
Dr. Kristina Olson is doing research on trans kids, following them for twenty years.

https://www.ucsfbenioffchildrens.org/clinics/child_and
_adolescent_gender_center/
Dr. Steven Rosenthal is the pediatric endocrinologist at UCSF Benioff Children's Hospital's Gender Center.

https://itspronouncedmetrosexual.com/2013/05/my-ted
-talk-understanding-the-complexities-of-gender/#sthash
.2E4AZpLt.dpbs

http://www.nbcbayarea.com/investigations/Transgender
-Kids-Eligible-for-Earlier-Medical-Intervention-Under
-New-Guidelines-423082734.html

STARSCAPE BOOKS
READING & ACTIVITY GUIDE
TO FREEING FINCH

by Ginny Rorby

Ages 10 & up; Grades 5 & up

About this Guide

The Common Core State Standards–aligned questions and activities that follow are intended to enhance your reading of *Freeing Finch*. Please feel free to adapt this content to suit the needs and interests of your students or reading group participants.

Synopsis of *Freeing Finch*

In a world that sometimes seems to be filled with more cruelty than compassion, sixth grader Morgan Delgado, Jr. (aka Finch) is coming to terms with her mother's death, her father's abandonment, "stand-in" parents, and being a transgender girl trapped in a boy's body. With the help of an animal-loving neighbor and a stray dog with wounds of his own, Finch discovers she has what she needs to survive, even to thrive. To do that, she must find the strength to choose healing over hurting, and the courage to live her own truth. On the wings of hope, she can fly beyond the dark past and her bittersweet present, if, as some poets imagine, hope is like a bird . . . maybe even a finch.

Pre-reading Discussion Questions

1. *Freeing Finch* explores some of the beauties and complexities of family, friendship, and accepting and expressing your individual identity. What is the biggest challenge you ever faced in one of these areas? How did you resolve it, or are you still working on it? Who helped, or is helping, you?

2. The main character in this story, sixth grader Morgan Delgado, Jr. (aka Finch), is a transgender girl. She identifies as a girl, but has the body of a boy. What is your understanding of gender identity, or what it means to be transgender?

3. In addition to exploring some of the mysteries of human nature, *Freeing Finch* also examines positive and negative interactions between people and animals (both wildlife and pets), including animals that have been injured, abused, or abandoned. The story's human protagonist, Finch, who has endured painful loss and rejection in her young life, develops a special connection with a stray dog (Ben) on a healing journey of his own. Have you observed, or heard or read about, a particularly positive or negative animal/human interaction? What did it inspire you to feel, think, or do?

4. In the novel *Freeing Finch* (as in real life), individuals and families are not one-size-fits-all. What do you think of as one of the most special, or unique, aspects of yourself? What are some unique family relationships you have experienced or observed (such as, stepparents or stepsiblings, multi-race families, adoptive or foster families, single parents, or same-gender parents)? Did they teach you something about yourself or others?

Post-reading Discussion Questions

1. Author Ginny Rorby includes this quote from writer and reformer Lillie Devereux Blake in the front matter of *Freeing Finch*: "People share a common nature but are trained in gender roles." How does this quote relate to the courageous, confusing, sometimes isolating, but ultimately liberating, journey, of the main character in *Freeing Finch*?

2. Ms. Rorby also includes this quote from author Robyn Davidson: "[The universe] gave us three things to make life bearable—hope, jokes and dogs. But the greatest of these was dogs." Discuss how this quote speaks to the intertwined stories of human protagonist Finch and the story's canine main character, Ben.

3. Why do you think the author chooses to reveal both of the main character's names—Morgan Delgado, Jr., and Finch—in the first two lines of the book? Do you think names and "labels" are significant in this story? Why? (Think about Morgan, Finch, Junior, "girl," "boy," and "Nancy-boy.")

4. Maddy says about the finch that hits Finch's and her mother's window: "The only thing wrong with this bird is she doesn't appreciate that you saved her life." Can this sentiment be applied to Finch, the human character, too? How, and in relationship to which other characters in the story?

5. In the closing lines of Chapter 1, Maddy says: "You're what you are in your head and heart, Finch, not what it says on your birth certificate." Does Finch believe this? What about her mother? Her father? How does the inability of some characters to embrace this notion cause conflict in Finch's home and school life?

6. Chapter 2 looks back at Finch at age five and a half, when Finch's mom receives her first cancer diagnosis. Throughout the book, the story shifts between the present and the past. Even sections within each chapter often move from one time or topic to a new one, with little transition. Why do you think the author chooses to structure the story in this way? How do the past events,

or memories, shape your understanding of Finch's present-day actions, attitudes, or feelings?

7. Why do you think Finch has an "idealized" vision of her absent father, in spite of his lack of empathy? How does Finch's attitude toward her father affect her feelings about her mother marrying her stepfather Stan, and then (later, after her mother passes away) about Stan marrying Cindee?

8. In Chapter 3, after asking Finch to please remove the fingernail polish Finch is wearing, Cindee says: "Be who God made you, okay?" Cindee has a particular view of God and religion. How does her point of view compare to Finch's? To Stan's? To Maddy's? How does this book explore differences between how people experience faith and spirituality, and the roles religion or nature can play in the experience?

9. Finch often spends time in the quiet spot between two redwoods, where she and Stan spread her mother's ashes after she passed away from cancer. Do you have a special place you like to go? Does it remind you of a significant time, place, or person?

10. In Chapter 3, Finch recalls being teased by Amanda Ellis when Finch was coming out of the handicapped bathroom, which she was required to use at Dana Gray Elementary because of her transgender status. How do Amanda's ignorance and intolerance play a central role in this story?

11. In Chapter 5, on her way back from a visit to the site of her mom's ashes, Stan asks if Mom "said" anything, and Finch wonders if Stan is making fun of her. Later, Finch is irritated when Cindee wants Finch to take a sweater and flashlight to Maddy's house. Does Finch misinterpret Stan's and Cindee's intentions in these, and other, instances? Can you recall other examples from the text, when (human or animal) characters misjudged or misunderstood each other?

12. After her fall from the roof, Maddy asks Finch to take care of her animals and the stray dog Maddy has started feeding. How does Finch's relationship with the dog (Ben) grow and change? How are their "stories" similar?

13. In Chapter 9, Finch introduces herself to Sherri Vines (a new student at school) as Finch, instead of Morgan. Why is this significant?

14. Why does Cindee want Finch to go to the summer camp for kids with gender identity "disorder"? Why can't, or doesn't, Finch believe that Stan and Cindee have Finch's best interests in mind?

15. As Finch and Sherri make plans for Halloween, Finch realizes she hasn't revealed to Sherri "all the truest and most important things about herself and her life." What does Finch's friendship with Sherri (and, later, her friendship with Gabe) teach Finch about the importance of trust, honesty, and vulnerability in friendship?

16. When they are trick-or-treating, Finch and Sherri encounter Sammy, a friend who knew Finch as a boy (before Finch started school as a girl). What is Sammy's reaction to seeing Finch as a girl? Why do people often respond to things they don't understand with fear or skepticism?

17. When Finch and Cindee pick Maddy up from Sherwood Oaks, Maddy and Cindee get into a tense discussion about God. Why does Cindee's inflexible attitude toward religion irritate Maddy?

18. After Stan discovers Finch's charge to a people-finder search engine, on Cindee's credit card bill, he gives Finch her father's contact information. Do you think he should have given it to Finch earlier? Why or why not?

19. What happens when Deanne, Sherri, and Finch make the trip to see Finch's father in Eureka? After Finch learns that her father left her and her mother because he couldn't handle the cancer and that he has a new family, she gets rid of all the keepsakes she's kept to remember him by. Finch also says: "I don't ever want to be called Morgan again. From now on, my name is Finch." What else is Finch letting go of, when she rejects her father's name/her birth name (Morgan)?

20. After she reveals her personal family history to Finch, Maddy says: "Now you and I are family." How does *Freeing Finch* explore the nature and meaning of family and home, and how can they be determined by more than biological connections? How does Stan and Cindee's relationship (which began as a way to give Finch a "home" and "family" after her mother passed away) develop into a love story of its own?

21. How does the Native American allegory (the tale of the two wolves), which Maddy shares with Finch, relate to the lives and struggles of key characters in *Freeing Finch*?

22. What happens when Cindee confronts Amanda Ellis's mom at the grocery store? What does Finch learn from this confrontation? What does Cindee learn?

23. After some high school boys attack Finch to see if she has "girl or boy parts," Finch starts to develop a friendship with Gabe. How does Gabe's revelation that he is gay affect Finch? How does Gabe help Finch after Ben is picked up by Animal Control?

24. In her author's note at the end of the book, Ginny Rorby shares her real-life observation of a dog walking a lonely path, and her inspirational interaction with Dr. Kathryn Rohr, who had the courage to pursue her true identity. Does it make you think of the book differently to know about these real-life inspirations for Finch and Ben's stories?

25. Why do you think the author chose the title *Freeing Finch*?

Common Core–aligned Reading Literature, Writing & Research Activities

These Common Core–aligned activities may be used in conjunction with the pre- and post-reading discussion questions above.

Gender Identity, Transgenderism & Genetics

1. In her journey to be accepted as a transgender daughter, friend, student, and individual, Finch encounters prejudice, ignorance, and misconceptions. As with most aspects of human development and identity, transgenderism is complicated. We can think about it emotionally, physically, logistically, and legally. We can also look at it scientifically, or genetically. Current scientific thinking holds that if a fetus is genetically a boy (contains an X and Y

chromosome), two waves of testosterone usually occur during fetal development to produce a boy body with a "boy brain" (or male gender identity). But sometimes either the earlier or later wave does not occur, which leads to a trans female (boy body, female gender identity) or trans male (girl body, male gender identity) individual. In a 1–2 page essay, state your opinion on whether you think educating people who are not transgender, about these genetic and scientific realities of transgenderism could help reduce the prejudice or skepticism some transgender individuals face. Why or why not? Or, write an opinion essay on why having this scientific knowledge could help people who are transgender better understand their emotional and physical experience. How and why might this knowledge be enlightening and empowering?

2. In *Freeing Finch*, Finch struggles to find acceptance and guidance as she tries to express her true gender identity, especially after she loses her empathetic mother to cancer. There are many resources available for transgender youth like Finch. Through online or library research, learn more about organizations, which support members of the LGBTQ (Lesbian, Gay, Bisexual, Trans, and Questioning) community. For example, you might check out: the National Center for Transgender Equality (transequality.org), and some of its programs, such as Voices for Trans Equality (VTE), and Families for Trans Equality (FTE); the Transgender Law Center (transgenderlawcenter.org); and the Trans Youth Equality Foundation (transyouthequality.org). Create an informational pamphlet or poster based on your research. Offer to leave pamphlets, or hang a poster, in your school library, guidance office, or cafeteria to help build awareness of the resources available to LGBTQ youth.

3. Invite students to work in pairs or small groups to do online and library research on one of the following subjects or concepts (or a topic of their choice) related to transgenderism: Gender Dysphoria; gender identity; gender expression; gender transition; gender confirmation surgery; gender variant or gender nonconforming; the North Carolina Bathroom Bill; transgender people in the military; a national, state, or local law regarding dis-

crimination against transgender people; how sexual-orientation discrimination laws, or Title IX protections, exclude or extend to transgender people; new, or developing, legal or medical policy, impacting issues specific to the transgender community. (**Hint:** The American Civil Liberties Union's website: aclu.org, has helpful sections on current language and laws relevant to the transgender community; and the organizations and websites listed in #2 above contain information on legal, medical, political, individual, and cultural activity and advocacy by and for the transgender community.) Use findings to inform a presentation to classmates. Have presentations serve as the basis for small group or classroom discussion. Students might also write short (independent) essays, summarizing what they learned on their topic.

4. Finch faces prejudice, bullying, and even physical attack because she is transgender; peers, family members, and even strangers, through their words or actions, hurt or judge, Finch just for trying to be herself. What can you and your peers do to make your own school or community more welcoming or inclusive? Consider organizing "Compassionate Conversation" discussion groups, to offer each other sensitive, constructive peer-to-peer support as you discuss issues of identity, self-expression, and self-advocacy. Or, invite friends or classmates to make "You Can" posters with positive imagery and inclusive, supportive slogans, such as: *At our school, YOU CAN Be True. Be You. Belong!; At our school, YOU CAN stand out without being shut out!* See how creative (and inclusive) YOU CAN get.

Story Structure, Themes, and Symbols

1. Sixth grader Morgan Delgado, Jr., or Finch, is the narrator of *Freeing Finch*. How might the story be different if it was told from another character's perspective? Have your students choose a significant event from the story (the death of Finch's mom; Maddy's fall; the scene where Stan drags Finch out of the bathroom; the trip to Eureka to see Finch's

father; the confrontation between Cindee & Amanda Ellis's mother at the store; the trip to Animal Control in
Ukiah, for example) and write a 2–3 paragraph description
of it from another character's (such as Maddy, Stan, Cindee, Sherri, Deanne, Amanda, or Gabe's) point of view.

2. *Freeing Finch* explores acceptance and intolerance, and
   choices and circumstances that can foster each of these
   mind-sets. Select a character from the story (such as
   Finch, Maddy, Finch's mother or father, Stan, Cindee,
   Amanda, Lacey, Sherri, or Gabe) and write an essay exploring how that character demonstrates acceptance or
   intolerance (or a bit of both). Be sure to cite specific dia-
   logue, actions, and examples from the text.

3. After she's injured, Maddy says: "I have to rehab my new
   hip. How's that for irony? I'm the critter with broken
   parts now." In both the title and text of *Freeing Finch*,
   animals are used to mirror, or symbolize, the hurt and
   healing human characters are experiencing (such as the
   house finch Maddy nicknames Finch for; (injured) Maddy
   and her wildlife; Rav the ornery hawk and Finch's grandfather; Ben and Finch). Citing relevant passages and
   details from the novel, write one or two paragraphs de-
   scribing an instance where an animal represents or
   reflects a human character. If you had to pick an animal
   symbol for yourself, which embodies aspects of your per-
   sonality or life story, which animal would you pick and
   why? Write 1–2 paragraphs explaining your choice.

4. In the book's front matter, author Ginny Rorby includes
   the following lines from Emily Dickinson's poem, "'Hope'
   is the thing with feathers": "'Hope' is the thing with
   feathers - That perches in the soul - " Look up the full
   text of the poem online or at the library. Similar to poet
   Emily Dickinson's choice to cast "hope" in the image of a
   bird, Ginny Rorby names Finch after a bird, who struggles, but survives. In a 1–2 page essay, discuss how the
   Dickinson poem's theme, imagery, and symbolism relate
   to *Freeing Finch*: How does the concept, purpose, and
   power of hope figure into this story? How does Maddy's
   description of the rescued (and ultimately released)
   female house finch, as a "voice with wings" echo Emily

Dickinson's poem? Can this description be applied to Finch, the human character, too? Why or why not? Be sure to cite relevant details, quotes, or passages from the novel, as you explore connections to the poem.

5. Inspired by the authenticity and artistry of Maddy's landscape paintings—and some of the key concepts in *Freeing Finch*—create a word collage, painting, or other work of art that explores your unique vision of "Self," "Gender," or "Family." Invite friends and classmates to produce their own works of art, for display in a "Lifescapes" art exhibit for your school or community.

Pet Rescue and Recovery

1. *Freeing Finch* explores the rescue, recovery, and rehoming of pets or animals that have been abused or abandoned, like Ben. The American Society for the Prevention of Cruelty to Animals (ASPCA) fights animal neglect and abuse on many fronts. Go to the library or online to learn more about these efforts. Create a PowerPoint presentation to share with classmates about the work of the ASPCA. (**HINT:** Check out aspca.org.)

2. After you have familiarized yourself with the mission and work of the ASPCA, write a 1–2 page essay, which explains why animal rights matter. Why and how should humans and laws protect animals? Draw upon examples from *Freeing Finch* in your essay (such as the house finch that crashes into Finch's and her mother's window; Maddy's rehabilitated "residents"—Otus the owl and Rav the red-shouldered hawk; the baby possum Finch helps; Ben, the abused and abandoned dog; and some of the other animals Finch and Gabe see when they visit Animal Control.)

Wildlife Rescue, Rehabilitation & Release

1. In *Freeing Finch*, Finch's neighbor and best friend (Maddy Baxter) has a permit from the California Department of

Fish & Wildlife to rehabilitate wildlife. Individuals like Maddy, with the time and space to help, can be great champions for wildlife. There are larger organizations dedicated to the cause, too. Do library or online research to learn more about some of these organizations and their work. **HINT:** Here are a few organizations to explore: National Wildlife Rehabilitators Association (nwrawildlife.org); Wildlife Rescue & Rehabilitation (wildlife-rescue.org); The Owl (Orphaned Wildlife) Rehabilitation Society (owlrehab.org); International Wildlife Rehabilitation Council (theiwrc.org). Use the research to create a PowerPoint or other multimedia style presentation to share findings with classmates.

2. In *Freeing Finch*, three of the main characters (Finch's environmentalist mother; animal-lover and rehabilitator Maddy; and Finch herself) share a deep respect for, and appreciation of, nature and wildlife. They often find peace and comfort in the natural world, in spite of its messiness and mystery. Finch's stepfather Stan, on the other hand, seems to want to tame and control nature with all the cutting and clearing he does in the forest. Look back through the book for passages, quotes, and moments that illustrate how these characters celebrate, or relate, to nature (or animals). Working in pairs or small groups, compare your examples and discuss if and how the histories and personalities of these characters might influence how they view nature, and their role in it.

The discussion questions and activities above support Common Core State Standards:

Reading Literature (RL): 5.1-4, 5.6; 6.1-4, 6.6; 7.1-2, 7.6; 9-10.1-3; 11-12.1-3; 11-12.5 Speaking & Listening (SL): 5.1, 5.4; 6.1, 6.4; 7.1, 7.4; 9-10.1A, 9-10.2, 9-10.4, 9-10.5; 11-12.1, 11-12.2, 11-12.4-5. Writing (W): 5.1-3, 5.7; 6.1-3, 6.7; 7.1-3, 7.7; 9-10.1-2A,B, 9-10.3, 9.10-7, 9-10.9; 11-12.1, 11-12.2A, 11-12.4, 11-12.7, 11-12.9.